A VERY MER–MERRY HOLIDAY

A VERY

MER-MERRY HOLIDAY

A SPARK OF LIFE NOVEL, BOOK FOUR

by

GINNA MORAN

ISBN 978-1-942073-89-5 (soft cover)
ISBN 978-1-942073-85-7 (ebooks)

Cover design by Silver Starlight Designs
Cover images copyright 123RF

For Inquiries Contact:
Sunny Palms Press
9663 Santa Monica Blvd Suite 1158
Beverly Hills, CA 90210, USA
www.sunnypalmspress.com
www.GinnaMoran.com

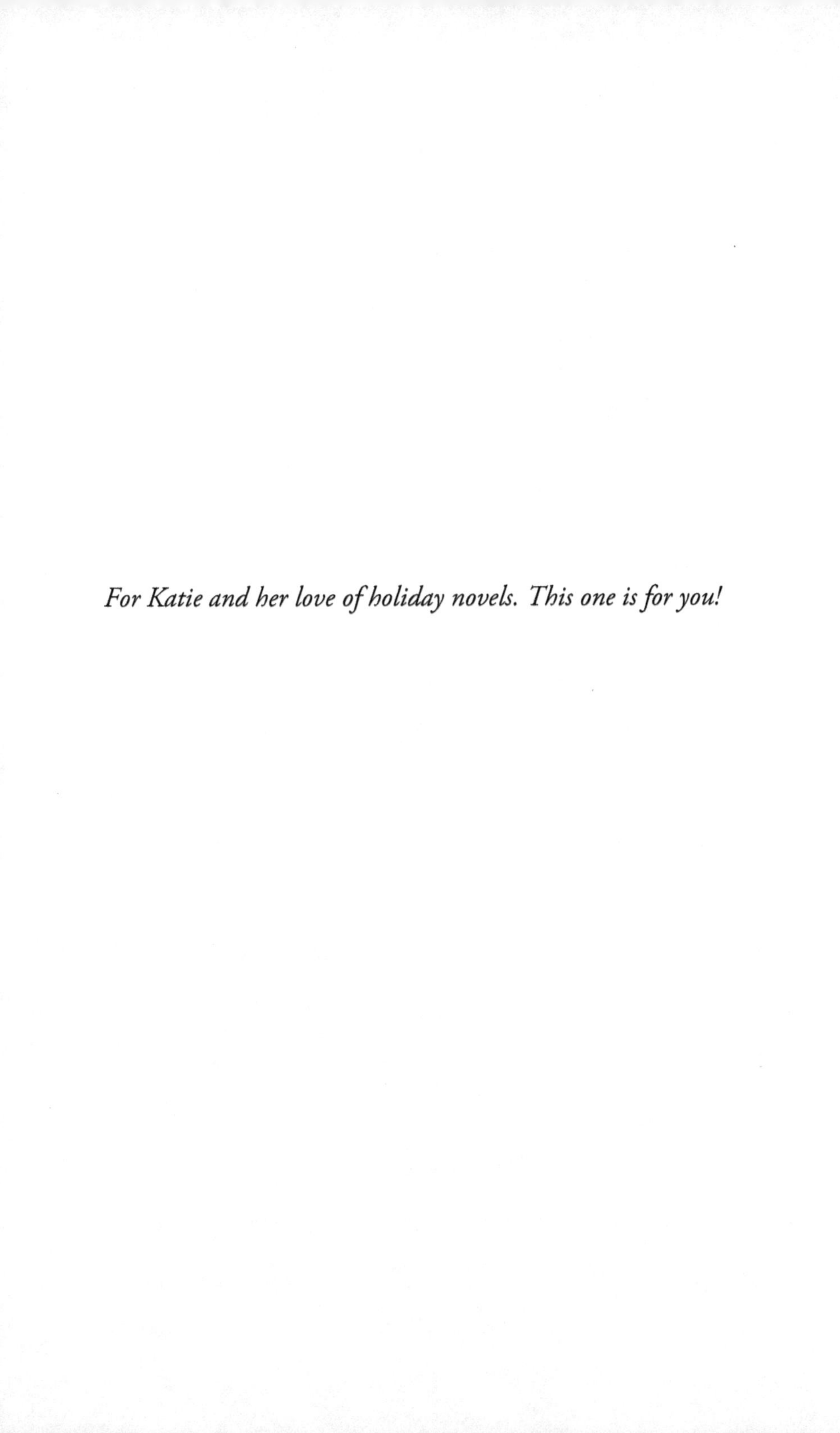

For Katie and her love of holiday novels. This one is for you!

1

A MER-MERRY CHRISTMAS

"I SWEAR IF I DIDN'T pass my final, I'm the worst—" I peer around the empty parking lot with direct access to the beach and whisper, "I'm the worst mermaid in the sea."

Carter chuckles, leaning against the short barred fence that separates the paved lot from the stretch of beach in walking distance from the lecture hall I took my last final exam at. He dangles a waterproof bag from his hand, his dark hair still dripping saltwater onto his forehead. His bluish-green eyes match the ocean behind him that turns into a brilliant gradient of blues when I stare at the clear horizon. "Or I'm the worst merman instructor."

"Possibly that, too," I say with a smirk as I slide my hands over his muscular shoulders and behind his neck to pull him in for a kiss. "Hard to concentrate with all the distractions."

I send him a dozen images from the final exam for my lecture simply called *The Ocean*, which should've been easy, all things considered. It took Carter swimming me all along the California coast to show me the ocean life up close and personal to go along with my professor's notes to even grasp the complexity of it all. I'm just glad it's over for now. I don't want to be a marine biologist or oceanographer, because I plan to own a bakery right next to Carter's future surf shop, but I'm doing it because I avoided the ocean for so long before Carter saved my life by turning me into a mermaid. I should get to know my home away from home a little better apart from giving fish my own names and snuggling against Carter as he swims me too fast to even take in the view.

Carter pulls away, raising an eyebrow, not expecting me to send what's probably the most boring memory I could ever share with him. "You passed. Don't worry. Now I can really distract you. All winter break."

I release a breath through my grin, squinting into the bright sunshine beating down from overhead. Tall palm trees cast shadows across the sand, and I pull him from his spot and guide him away in the opposite direction of the long pier and aquarium that's just down the beach. We've become familiar with these shores over the last few months since I started my fall semester of college. I swim on the days my best friend, Giselle, doesn't have class to avoid the nightmarish parking situation. And today, since Giselle finished her last final already, I took the easy way and swam from home.

"You know, I can call in sick tonight and swim us anywhere if you want to celebrate surviving your first semester. Travis wouldn't mind. The shop has been dead all week because of the holidays." Carter watches me in the corner of his vision. He managed to get a job as a surf instructor/manager at the Big Swell Surf School and Shop near our condo, which we share with Giselle in La Tortuga Point. It doesn't pay as much as the Ocean Jewel, the yacht we met on, did, but it's flexible and allows us to travel without much notice when someone needs me at one of the merpeople colonies.

"You have no idea how much I want to go, but I promised my parents I'd have dinner with them, remember? I haven't seen them in two weeks." We stroll hand in hand on the stretch of beach in front of a community of mansions not unlike the one I used to live in with my parents in Azure Waters. This time of year, the ocean is freezing, so we don't have to worry about too many beachgoers, and once we hit the water, our mer essences will prevent humans from seeing us. But the playful colony of seals that reside along the beach here is another story.

Carter bumps his shoulder with mine. "What's another day?"

I laugh, shaking my head. My blond hair smacks my

cheeks, and I nudge him toward the surf. "Fine, but you have to be the one to call my dad and tell him."

Carter grimaces, making me laugh again. While my parents have taken the whole me transforming into a mermaid thing in stride, they're still getting used to the fact that I've basically eloped under the sea with a boy I only knew for weeks at the time. They're coming around, but it's been an adjustment knowing that I go places they'll never be able to follow.

"I take that as a no?" I ask. I rest my hand on Carter's shoulder to shimmy out of my jeans right in the sand.

He folds my clothes and sticks them into his waterproof bag along with my purse, and then trails his eyes from my face to my toes to take in my navy blue, halter top bikini. If I hadn't picked a school in a beach city, it might have gotten some side-eyes that I'm always dressed for a swim, but a lot of people do it here. I've even seen people cross campus in wetsuits.

"It might be worth it," he says, scooping me into his arms before I have a chance to brace myself. Cool water splashes over me, making me shiver in my human form. Carter carries me until the waves wash over my head and then he dives us into the freezing Pacific.

Calming silence greets me in the current that pulls us farther from shore. With a gentle tug of his fingers, Carter unlaces my bikini bottoms. I wait until my lungs start to burn, just floating half-naked in the bubbling sea for a moment, before I will my transformation to take hold. Cramps pulse in my legs and seize my back but then warmth blossoms from the spark lighting my chest to travel through the rest of me. I inhale a long breath of saltwater, filling up every inch of me with the ocean that picked me for Carter.

Opening my eyes, I peer around and meet Carter's sparkling aqua eyes, the color of the sea around us. He closes the distance, sliding his fingers through my flowing hair, and just smiles at me. Tiny bubbles cling to his pearlescent tan skin and dark hair. He leans forward, kissing me like he always does after a transformation, and I slide my arms around him, feeling the strength of his fin jet us through the shallows, dodging around overly friendly seals who want nothing more than to play with us.

It's only been a few hours since I last swam, but diving under and exploring the familiar shore is comparable to changing into pajamas and plopping on the couch after a long day of being out. It feels like home.

Carter's muscular chest presses into my back, and I hold my arms in front of us, pretending that I'm flying through the water. The shadow of a boat crawls across the glittering sand in front of us, and I wave my hand, creating a magical current strong enough to push all the fishing lines out of our way.

A few of the lines tangle together, and Carter chuckles in my mind. "You just love annoying the fishermen, don't you?"

I grin even though he can't see my face. "What kind of mermaid would I be if I didn't?"

"Still an amazing one," he thinks to me.

I shake my head, rolling my eyes, though I love when he

says what Giselle calls "grossly cute things" to me. He's reeled it in a lot on land, keeping all the gushy stuff between us, but when we're in the sea and he's in his true form, he can't help himself. The tides might be changing in the merpeople world, but a mate's bond is something that'll stay the same—unending and irrevocable. I could never deny his affection, even if I tried, not that I would.

Slowing down, Carter swims along the sandy floor and into the familiar shallows of Azure Waters. A loan surfer sits on a board, waiting for a swell, and I push myself away from Carter and in her direction.

I break through the surface and spit water right into Giselle's face. She screams, falling off her board and into the surf where I grab onto her and pop us back up into the cool, wintery air. Carter splashes up next to us, and Giselle gets him in the face with a wave of water intended for me.

She laughs and splashes me next. "You owe me an awesome swell for that, Aves."

"That was for waking me at sunrise this morning," I say.

Giselle and Carter have taken up early morning surfing with our other friend Chloe at least twice a week, even in the cold water. I don't even know how they can enjoy waking up with the sun, because I'd sleep in all day if I could. Not like anyone ever lets me.

Giselle pops back onto her board. "I was going to apologize, but I'm not even sorry."

"I guess you enjoy calm waters, huh?" I ask, jokingly. I'd

never hear the end of it if I used my mermaid magic to kill my best friend's surf fun.

"Ava!" a voice calls out from the beach, drawing my attention away from Giselle and Carter.

Raising my hand, I wave to my sister, Bailey, who stands on the small patio of the remodeled sea green Victorian mansion I used to call home. I dip back under, leaving Giselle on her board on the surface, and change back into my human form. Carter hands me my bikini bottoms, and I put them on before kicking to the surface to clear my lungs.

"Get ready, Gi," I say. With a wave of my hand, I create a swell that drags the three of us to the beach to meet my sister.

She greets me right in the surf and hugs me, something I'll never take for granted. I wasn't sure we'd ever have a good relationship after being apart for so many years, but I'm so thankful she's come around since returning home to live with our parents.

"That was unexpected," I say with a smile, pulling away from Bailey.

She shrugs her shoulders and nods to Carter. "I'm just glad you're here. Mom and Dad are acting really weird. All secretive and overly excited. Something is up."

I turn my gaze to Giselle. "Do you know something?"

She grins, nodding her head. "I promised my mom I wouldn't say anything."

"Should I be scared?" I ask.

"Definitely."

I glare, but she only smirks and pretends to lock her lips closed with an invisible key. Carter hooks his hands to my waist from behind, nudging me forward, and the four of us head to the glass door that'll lead to the entertainment room of my parents' house.

Bailey passes us all towels from the cabinet near the door, and warm air pushes away the goosebumps prickling over my skin. Going from my mermaid to human form in icy water is probably my least favorite thing, and I'm already dreaming of the summer sun.

"Oh, Carter, I'm so glad you could stop by with Avie. Are you staying for dinner?" Mom says from the doorway leading to the rest of the house.

"Can't. I'm closing the store tonight but wanted to make sure Ava made it here after class," he says.

Mom beams a smile, not because he can't stay, but most likely because Carter always knows exactly what to say in front of my parents to let them know they never have to worry about me. "Come in the kitchen. I'll pack you a few things to go. Plus, I don't want you to miss the announcement. You're part of the family, too."

Announcement? Now I'm starting to get a little freaked out. Bailey purses her lips, giving me a told-you-so face. All I can do is shrug and stroll next to Carter behind the others as Mom leads us into the kitchen.

Wes, Bailey's mate, sets utensils on placemats at the kitchen table and greets us with a smile. Dad stands at the six burner stove, stirring what smells like my grams' beef stew, and he waves a wooden spoon in our direction.

The overly excited smile on Mom's face has me antsy to find out the big announcement. I'm almost afraid they're going to tell us they've decided to retire early and move to some Caribbean island. Though the ocean would be the perfect temperature all year round, I fought too hard to return to Azure Waters to just have them up and leave me.

"Carter can't stay, so I thought we could tell them the surprise now," Mom says before any of us can even sit down.

"Yes, please. Now. You guys are freaking me out," I say.

Dad laughs. "Can't be any worse than—" He turns his gaze to Carter, thinking better than to talk about how I kind of just threw the whole mermaid thing at them without much warning after vanishing while pretending to be traveling.

"We're going on a Christmas vacation!" Mom says, throwing her hands up like she's bursting with imaginary confetti.

Giselle claps her hands. "To Australia! We're getting another yacht and are going to sail around the Whitsundays. Everyone's going. It's going to be a blast."

I'm not sure what my parents were expecting, but I'm sure it wasn't the silence coming from the rest of us. Bailey and Wes share a look like they want nothing to do with a Christmas vacation on an island, and who can blame them after spending the last eight years worth of holidays imprisoned on an island by the ocean. And Carter, he doesn't do the whole Christmas thing. He celebrates Winter Solstice with all the other merpeople colonies, because it's the longest night of the year, and this year is extra special because of the full moon.

"Um, that sounds great and all, but—"

"Ava," Mom says, cutting me off. "This is the first Christmas we're finally together again as a family."

Uh oh. I'm pretty sure if I even utter a single complaint, I'll be forever the destroyer of Adair holidays, but if I don't, I'm about to become the ruiner of mermaid traditions. The killer of all things special about this time of year. The most—

"We'll be there," Carter says, speaking up for me.

Mom motions us all in for a group hug, and I close my eyes, trying to calm the panic washing through my heart. This is what I've always wanted, to be able to celebrate during Christmas instead of grieving, feeling the absence of Bailey.

And after seeing how happy my parents are, I'm pretty sure Bailey's already over the dissatisfaction of an island destination, because the adventure this time will be a million times better. She won't have to fear the sea, not with me around.

We all break apart, and I lace my fingers through Carter's. "Want me to walk you out?" I ask, practically dragging him toward the game room before he can answer, leaving Mom gushing all the details to the others.

The second the back door clicks closed and the hum of the waves drowns out all other noise, I jab my finger into Carter's bare chest. "Why did you agree? You said Winter Solstice was a big deal."

"And risk your family hating me for ruining their holiday?"

he asks.

"Yeah, but now I'll have all the colonies hating *me.*" I take a breath. "It's Summer Solstice there. Luna said everyone travels to Pearlestria to celebrate in the northern hemisphere, and I doubt we could just leave and not be missed by my family."

Carter reaches up and pushes my hair behind my ears, cupping my cheeks between his hands. "We'll make it work. Stop freaking out."

"I just—it's a lot of pressure."

"We'll be fine."

"You say that now—"

Carter interrupts me with a kiss, sending me a dozen images that calm my racing heart, because freaking out over a holiday vacation is nothing compared to all the stuff we survived together. "Come on, Aves. Relax. It'll be a mer-merry Christmas. You'll see."

I snort, batting his shoulder. "You're something else."

"Something good, I hope."

I laugh. "You better go now before I convince you to stay."

He slowly pulls away. "I'll call in sick."

I shake my head. "Not now with our surprise vacation you aren't. Plus, I don't want to be within phone-passing reach when you call and tell your mom."

He grimaces. "I'll call Dad."

I kiss him once more. "And I'll be turning my phone off."

"Careful, she might swim here."

I roll my eyes. "I'll take my chances."

2

CHANGE OF PLANS

A KNOCK SOUNDS ON THE bedroom door, stirring me from sleep. Carter moans next to me, but doesn't open his eyes. Instead, he curls his arm around me and pulls me closer. I lie against him for a few seconds, peeking around our still dark room. I swear if Giselle is at the door with her surfboard, she'll not have waves for a week.

"Go away!" I call. "You surfed yesterday."

"You better get your ass up. There's a flustered mermaid pacing on our back patio," Giselle says through the door. "I'm not facing her first."

I shove Carter a few times, rocking him on the bed. "Get up. Your mom is here."

Carter snaps his eyes open. "Did she knock?"

"No," Giselle says, cracking the door open. "But she's going to draw attention."

"She'll leave before she does. Just ignore her," he says.

I smack him on the shoulder. "Seriously?"

"I warned you when you told me to call her."

Groaning, I slide my legs over the side of our bed and push to my feet. I throw a pillow at Carter for good measure and meet Giselle in the hall. Carter flips on his stomach, ignoring the heated glare I burn at him as I close the door. Sure, he only got home a few hours ago because his boss decided to do last minute inventory since the store was dead, but I waited up for him, and we went for a late night swim.

Giselle follows behind me, probably more for Starla's protection than mine. The mermaid did save her life once, but Giselle might also be making sure we don't wake up our whole community. Even though Starla and I are on mostly good terms, she still loves to question my decisions. Since she's hanging out on my patio at five in the morning, I'm sure she has a lot to say about Winter Solstice.

Giselle heads into our open kitchen and flicks on the under cabinet lights, setting our small living room aglow. I pull back the blinds on our slider, staring at Starla's back as she faces the waves crashing on the beach a few dozen feet away. If it wouldn't flood our condo, I'd consider summoning a tidal wave to wash her back out to sea so I could go back to sleep and worry about her later. But of course, I'd never hear the end of that either.

I flick on the patio light and unlock the door, drawing her attention to me. "Is everything all right, Starla? Did something happen?" I block her entrance into our living room by crossing my arms and leaning on the doorframe.

She purses her lips, because we both know why she's standing at my door, but I'm going to play stupid for as long as I can. "Everything's fine. I just wanted to come by in person to—"

"Who wants coffee?" Giselle asks from the kitchen, interrupting Starla. She knows I'll try to keep the conversation short and between us, but Giselle can't resist butting in.

Sighing, I motion for Starla to come in and close the door. "Carter's asleep if you're wondering. He worked a late shift."

"Actually, I came to talk to you." She adjusts the sarong around her waist. I still can't figure out how she manages to look so pretty coming straight from the sea. Whenever she comes to visit, she never brings more than a small bag, and more often than not, leaves Mateo, Carter's dad, in San Francisco.

"To me? What for?" I tilt my head, still playing dumb. Giselle smirks at me as she hands over two cups of coffee and some creamer.

Starla takes a sip of hers, drinking it black. "The Winter Solstice. Carter mentioned your family invited you on some sort of vacation..."

"Yeah, it's our first one together as a fam—"

"You have to cancel, Ava," she says, cutting me off. "You have a responsibility to our people. Pearlestria's been planning for weeks. This isn't like skipping out on the holidays because you don't want to hang out with your in-laws. This is like canceling them altogether. Think of all the merbabes you'll be disappointing. They all look forward to this. It's tradition."

"Damn, Aves. Carter turned you into the Grinch. You're lucky you can't see merbabes crying underwater." Giselle's lucky I can't summon a wave indoors. Like she'd even know that information. The only merbabe she's met was Carter's nephew, and he wouldn't even swim close enough for her to cuddle.

I glare at Giselle. "I'm not trying to ruin things, but I can't cancel, Starla."

"Ava."

I hold my hands up. "Wait. Before you go shouting that I'm the slayer of Winter Solstice, which you can thank Carter for because he's more scared of my dad hating him than he is of you hating me, just hear me out. I was thinking we could celebrate in Reefaria instead. It's the closest colony to where we're heading."

"But it's the shortest night of the—"

"We'll switch off this year. Sort of like Christmas in July for the Southern Hemisphere's Winter Solstice. I think Reefaria would be excited to host both holidays," I say. I don't actually know that, but what I do know is that merpeople can adapt, and quickly, something the former king didn't want them to do.

"I don't know," Starla says, leaning her elbows on the counter.

"This way, you and Mateo could also celebrate a human Christmas with us, too. You know, as one big happy blended family." I hold my breath, hoping it's enough to get Starla to relax. The most important thing to merpeople is their bonds, and second to a mate is the one they share with their pod— their family. They don't separate the relationships like humans. Starla fully believes me to be her daughter no matter how much of a pain in the ass she thinks I am.

Her face softens and a smile crosses her mouth. "Oh, Carter didn't mention that."

Because they technically weren't invited... "Did you give him a chance?"

Giselle turns away, trying to contain herself knowing full well I'm making stuff up as I go to get Starla to calm down and agree. I'm sure my parents won't mind. If it came down to having me around for Christmas or adding a couple extra people to our vacation, they'd probably invite every merperson in the sea...which they might have to.

Tapping her fingers on the bar, Starla's quiet for a long moment. "I think we can make this work. There's still time for everyone to travel to Reefaria, but you'll have to make the official announcement as soon as you can."

"Okay, I can manage that," I say, standing. "Now if you

don't mind, I need to get some sleep if I'm going to have to swim to Pearlestria. You're welcome to stay of course."

"I can make some breakfast or something," Giselle says, speaking up.

Starla nods. "I'd like that. Thanks."

"I can't believe you're making me tell your parents," Giselle says, crossing her arms. She stands next to me with the bright sun shining overhead, creating streaks of copper in her hair.

"You know how weird they get when I bring up the whole—" I lean into her. "The whole secret life of a mermaid queen," I whisper. "It's easier for them if it comes from someone who isn't me or Carter."

"What about Bailey or Wes?" she asks.

"Come on, Gi. You know Bailey doesn't like to talk about that stuff either. Please." I bump my hip to hers.

She twists her lips to the side. "Only if I get a personal tour of the Great Barrier Reef or something on vacation."

"Done."

"And a really amazing Christmas present."

"Whatever you want."

"A merman."

"Within reason."

She sighs. "Then surprise me."

I hug my best friend, rocking her back and forth until she laughs. Voices sound from our condo and Carter and Starla stroll into the sand. Pulling away from Giselle, I turn toward my mate. Carter slides his arm over my shoulders and kisses the top of my head like he's missed me even though we've spent the morning together hiding in our room until Giselle couldn't handle Starla's company any longer.

"All set?" he asks, looking between me and Giselle.

Giselle jabs him in the shoulder with her finger. "You owe me, dude. Like big time."

Carter chuckles. "Give me a list."

She smiles. "It'll be on the fridge when you guys get back. I'm really going to enjoy this Christmas vacation."

Rolling my eyes, I pull Carter forward with me and into the lapping surf. Starla says goodbye to Giselle before turning to us. "You sure you don't want me to go with you?"

Carter glances at me and then to Starla. "For the hundredth time, we have this under control. Go home. Get everything set at the store, and we'll see you in a few days."

"Call me when you return to shore, Ava," Starla says.

I force myself to nod and smile. "Got it. Now, have a good swim, okay? Next time just call. You don't have to keep dropping everything for me."

"But you're family."

"And you worry too much."

She puffs out a small breath through her lips like she's going to argue. Instead, she wraps her arms around us with me squished in the middle and then steps into the surf. Wading into the calm water, she looks once around the empty beach and dives into a wave. Carter and I stand on the beach until we can no longer see her form in the sand-clouded sea.

I peer around the quiet beach, the almost white sand glittering in the sunlight. It's been months since I've just got to hang out and relax out here without stressing over studying and exams, and now I can't even do that. So much for an actual break.

Carter's fingers lace through mine, drawing my attention away from the sand. Giselle stands on the other side of him, pouting her lip at me like she knows what's going through my head, which she does. We were supposed to just lay out on the beach today before mermaid obligations got in the way. It's something we haven't gotten to do much over the last eight years because I was so afraid of the ocean. I have a lot of catching up to do.

"Think you'll be back tonight?" Giselle asks, filling the silence. "Sapphire and Matty are coming in from LA. Thought we could go to the Taco Palace."

I shrug. "Hopefully. I don't want to stay longer than I have to. I already need a vacation before our vacation."

She laughs. "Hey, just be thankful we're not still stuck on a desolate island."

Too true.

With one last hug from Giselle, I let Carter pull me forward and into the waves. The freezing water sends a shiver down my back, and we dive to swim deep enough to transform without hanging out in our human forms for long because of the temperature.

Sucking in a cool breath of ocean water, I push it out of my gills and blink to adjust my eyes to the murky sea this close to shore. Carter swims circles around me, spinning me in a current of his making before catching me in his arms for a kiss. He sends a dozen memories to me from this morning, and I grin, nuzzling my nose to his when I break free.

With me in his arms, Carter jets from the shallows, through long, slimy strands of seaweed beds, and into the open ocean. His heart beats against mine in the same perfect rhythm, and I just enjoy feeling his arms around me as the aquatic world blurs by. We've swam from our condo to the colony of Pearlestria a dozen times since classes started, but Carter can't stop himself from swimming his fastest, never letting me take in the ocean in between. I won't ask him to slow down now, either, because I really want to make it home for dinner. If only my thoughts could reach the colony from the shore.

"Do you think everyone's going to hate me for switching things up?" I ask, running my fingers over Carter's shoulders since he still hasn't repositioned me to ride on his back.

"They could never hate you, Aves," he thinks, his thoughts reflecting his own loving feelings for me. He's definitely biased in how he thinks others see me because of how he sees me.

"What if the ocean makes me renounce my mermaid essence?"

"Now you're being ridiculous. It's one holiday, and we're still celebrating."

I pout my lip. "Merbabes are going to cry."

Bubbles erupt from Carter's mouth as he laughs out loud. "At least you can't see the tears."

I bat his chest, pushing away from him. He doesn't let me get far and just flips me over onto his back, locking his hands with mine. His back muscles ripple under my chest, tightening and loosening with each flick of his strong fin. He dives down to avoid a school of silver fish that look like a glittering cloud underwater.

My eyes adjust at the change of light the deeper we descend, and bubbles prickle over every inch of me as we enter the magical waters surrounding Pearlestria in all its shimmering beauty. A pearlescent wall winds the outskirts of the small colony. From here, sunbeams bounce off the shimmering castle encrusted with breathtaking jewels. Merpeople swim around the main sand channel with large houses made of glittering rock on either side. Among them are an array of tropical fish of all shapes and sizes that inhabit the coral and ocean within the stunning colony.

"Ava! Carter!" A few merpeople call our names, probably surprised to see us here so early. The atmosphere has changed since my last visit, and it even feels more festive. A huge rock platform sits in the sand outside the castle. Long ropes of kelp, braided together, twist up from each corner and almost look tree-like with shells and sea glass strung within the braids.

"Princess Luna," someone calls. "The queen is here."

"What?" I hear Luna before I see her. "Ava? We weren't expecting you for another week."

Luna jets from the main archway of the castle, past the single guard on post, not that anyone really needs protecting. It's more for order, I guess, since the whole colony might accidentally hug me to death or something with their excitement.

I open my arms. "Surprise..."

Before she interrogates me, she greets me with a hug and a kiss on both my cheeks. Her black hair drifts through the water between us, and she pushes it behind her ears. She gazes at me, her dark sapphire eyes crinkling in the corners, and then she smiles, showing off her straight, slightly pointed teeth.

"What are you two doing here?" she asks, glancing between me and Carter.

My stomach knots with nerves. Maybe telling my family I have to bail on them is better than telling an ocean of merpeople that we'll be celebrating Summer Solstice in Reefaria instead of Winter Solstice at the castle.

"Well," I say, wishing Luna would let go of my hands so she can't feel them trembling.

She definitely feels them, because her gaze drops to our fingers, and she frowns. "Is everything okay? Celestiana Cove? Is my dad—"

"No, he's fine," I say, though I don't really know. I haven't been to what I like to call the adjustment island for merpeople who want to explore the land without immersing themselves into a human society quite yet in a while. "But I've come because there's been a change of plans. My family is going on vacation for Christmas in Australia, and I can't miss it. It's our first one with Bailey since we were kids and—"

Her mouth drops open. "But Winter Solstice is here."

I push a bubble through my lips and glance to Carter for help.

"We want to move things to Reefaria," Carter says for me. "It's too hard for us to travel between the two places in such a short time."

"And I figured we could celebrate Winter Solstice there in June."

"But they're not equipped to handle such celebrations," she says.

I squeeze her hands. "I'm sure we can make things work. We'll go early to help out. It'll be fun."

The face she gives me, all twisted lips and puckered brows, clearly shows her doubt. It's enough to make me doubt my own plan. "Is this really what you want?"

"I just want to spend the holidays with my whole family. I bet we can find some uninhabited islands nearby and we can blend some traditions. It'll be great. Promise," I say. *Damn it.* I shouldn't have promised in case things suck, and I do end up being the destroyer of Winter Solstice.

"Okay then. I'll send Tide out to inform all the colonies, and I'll head to Reefaria with you first thing in the morning," she says.

"The morning?"

"There's so much to do to get things ready on time."

I pull her into a hug. "Okay, morning it is. And thank you

so much for helping. I don't know what I'd do without you."

She smiles. "What are friends for?"

MAKE IT WORK

LUNA SPITS WATER OVER MY head, her musical laughter tinkling through the air against the dull hum of the lapping night surf. "Whoa, it's so cold!"

I laugh through my chattering teeth. "At least the water will be w-warm in Australia, right?"

Carter pops up next to me, sending a small wave over my head. I duck back under to avoid getting knocked away.

Warm hands hook to my sides, pulling me back to the surface. Carter greets me with a wide smile. The waxing moon reflects silver light into his blue-green eyes, casting his dark tan skin in a soft glow. Treading water to stay afloat, I brush my lips to his cheek while reaching for the bag on his shoulder.

"You can wear my bottoms, Luna." I hand over my bikini bottoms to her from the bag. I hadn't planned on Luna coming to shore or else I'd have brought something for her to wear.

"What are you going to wear, Aves?" Carter asks.

I grin. "Your shorts. The beach is empty and the light is off in the condo. You can manage."

He narrows his eyes at me and crinkles his nose in a fake glare. He could just ask me to return to the water with something for him, but he couldn't care less about stepping onto the beach in all his bare, Olympic swimmer's body goodness. I'm not going to complain about that one either, even with Luna here, because she doesn't look at Carter any other way than him being my mate.

"Anything for you, Aves," he whispers, running his hand lower down my side to squeeze my hip bone.

Luna releases a small coo-like noise. "I can't wait to find my mate. You two are so cute."

"Tell Giselle that," I say, laughing. "She thinks we're gross most of the time."

"Love is not gross. Human's are so weird," she says.

I laugh again. "That's what she says about us."

Luna and I get dressed, and we all swim to the shore. My knees hit the sand, and a wave knocks me onto my stomach. It takes me a moment to orient myself because now I'm shivering uncontrollably. Carter and I have talked about visiting the colony near Greenland again, but I could never imagine transforming into a human near the North Pole no matter how much I'd love to waddle with the penguins on the ice. That would be some Winter Solstice if my parents decided on a frozen instead of tropical Christmas.

Carter helps me to my feet and then helps Luna to hers. We jog through the sand and to the back patio of the condo. I pull the key for the slider from the combination lock box on the wall and open the door, allowing Carter to enter our living room first.

A high-pitched whistle sounds through the air, and I hustle inside to see Sapphire, Matty, and Giselle hanging out in our dark living room with just the glow of the TV. "Dude, do you always just come straight from the waves like this?" Matty asks, cracking up.

Sapphire covers her mouth with her hand, trying not to look at Carter. "Well, this was an interesting merpeople welcome for us."

I reach into the chest where we keep towels near the door and hand one to Carter, who doesn't even attempt to cover up while he drips water all over the floor. I've grown used to his brazen attitude about being nude, but I know my friends haven't. At least they think it's hysterical.

I grab another two towels, handing one to Luna. "I didn't think anyone was home since we're late."

"Matty's been complaining for an hour, but I wanted to

wait for you guys," Giselle says. "And I'm glad I did."

Sapphire smirks. "Me, too."

I roll my eyes. "I hope you don't mind that Luna crashes here tonight."

Giselle gets to her feet and crosses the room. "Of course not. I'm excited you brought my mer-partner in crime."

Luna giggles and hugs Giselle. "I brought you and Ava both something." Reaching to the back of her neck, Luna unties the two necklaces she's wearing made from what looks like some fishing line, sea glass, and sea shells. She hands one to each of us. "I hope you like them."

"Love them," Giselle says. "It's like early Christm—Winter Solstice?"

I let Carter tie the necklace around my neck. "It's beautiful. Thank you."

"This is sweet to watch and all, but can you guys get dressed already so we can get some food?" Matty asks from his spot on the couch.

Sapphire slaps his arm. "Says the guy who just ate an entire bag of chips."

"I feel you, man. Been swimming for a few hours," Carter says, crossing the room. "Why don't you three go ahead without us and order, and we'll meet you there? That way food's ready and waiting."

Matty fist bumps Carter from the couch. "Good deal. I'll order double the usual."

"I bet we could eat triple," I say.

Matty raises an eyebrow. "I'll take that bet. Loser buys."

"Deal," I say.

Matty groans, standing from the couch and offers his hand out to help Sapphire. Giselle follows them to the front door, grinning once at me, and leaves me alone with Carter and Luna. I motion for Luna to step toward the hallway.

"You can use Giselle's bathroom. Towels are in the cupboard, and I'll put some clothes on her bed," I say.

"Something warm," she says.

I nod. "Definitely no dresses." It's taken me months to switch from dresses to pants, because of my lingering fear of needing to get out of my clothes quickly, but now that I'm pretty sure I have things under control, I've expanded my wardrobe options.

After setting out a pair of jeans I bought especially for Luna since her legs are longer than mine and a sweater, I head to my room to grab my own clothes. My cell lights up from my nightstand, and I see a few missed calls from both my mom and Starla.

I consider ignoring them to join Carter in the shower, but my phone buzzes in my hand. Sighing, I answer with, "Hey, Mom. What's up?"

"I just wanted to catch up with you about vacation. Giselle said that you invited Carter's parents." My mom breathes into the phone. She doesn't sound mad or anything, thankfully.

I plop on my bed still wearing my damp bikini and Carter's shorts. "I hope that's okay. You see, the Winter—well,

I guess now—Summer Solstice is a major holiday for merpeople, and it's something I can't just skip out on."

"But you're still coming with us, right?"

"Well, yes and no—"

"Avie," Mom says, cutting me off. "I know things are different now, but I'm really trying to make this all work. We're your family—"

"They're my family, too. And I said I'd be there. I just have to go early to get things—"

She sighs. "Maybe we can add a few days and come with you."

"I'm swimming," I say.

"All the way to Queensland?"

"Closer to New Zealand. It'll take a few days."

"But flying is—"

"Mom." I suck in a deep breath through my nose. I know she worries about me, especially after everything, and I know she's terrified that one day I just won't return to shore, but she's turning into Starla, and one overbearing woman is enough in my life.

"Mom," I say again. "I know you really want us to travel together, but I'm not sure I can survive such a long flight."

"Why not?"

I close my eyes, trying to stop myself from replying with something snarky. In moments like these, I'm glad I'm out of the house, because I don't know how I'd deal. It's much easier for my friends to understand, but they were never responsible for my wellbeing, and I know it bothers both my parents that they can't take care of me like they used to. I thought having Bailey home would help, but Bailey's been so self reliant for years that she doesn't exactly need them either.

My phone beeps in my hand, and silence settles between us because I can't bring myself to answer my mom's question. I glance at my screen. *Speaking of another overbearing woman. Ugh.*

Covering my face with my hand, I take another deep breath, trying to settle the stress washing over me.

"Ava, are you still there?"

Tingles rush up my legs, stealing my answer away. I rub my hands over my knees for a moment, trying to push them away. But then a series of cramps grips my lower back, sending me bolting to my feet. It's been so long since something triggered my transformation, I almost missed the signs. And now I'm terrified.

"I'll call you back, Mom." I drop my phone on my bed and rush to the door, flinging it open. It clatters against the wall with a bang, but I don't stop. I bolt down the short hallway and to the living room where I exit the glass slider onto our back patio and the beach.

Thank the ocean I didn't take my mom's call at dinner or else I'd be a mermaid out of water in the middle of a busy restaurant. The fact that a transformation is unexpectedly coming cements my decision to avoid over half a day in the air when my tail belongs in the water.

Tears burn my eyes, and it feels like the first time I accidentally triggered a transformation all over again. I can't help but think that maybe this is karma for changing up a long held tradition for mermaids. What if I'm being punished for failing as the ocean-chosen queen?

I kick into a wave, pushing through another series of cramps. "Why is this happening?"

I half expect a verbal answer, but all I'm greeted with is an icy swell that knocks me over and drags me into the surf. The easy thing for me to do would be to submit to the sea, take a calm breath of saltwater, and then transform back, but I'm angry I'm being forced to transform against my will.

"Are you angry with me?" Again, my question goes unanswered.

The roar of the sea hums in my ears, and I wave my hand and send a wave toward the open water, disturbing the surf. The rocky water pushes me around for a moment and becomes too rough that I have no choice but to dive.

Squeezing my eyes shut, I concentrate on calming my rapid heartbeat along with the water until things return to normal. With a deep breath of water, I complete my transformation and swim a few dozen feet away from the shore before popping to the surface.

"Aves?" Carter calls from the patio, a fluffy towel wrapped around his waist.

The moment he sees me, he jogs through the sand, leaving the towel on shore and swims to me in his human form without transforming despite the chill in the water. He cups my face in his hands, pulling me closer to keep us together in the slow-moving current, and gazes into my eyes with a pout.

"What are you doing out here?" he asks when he realizes I'm not going to say anything.

A tear trickles onto my cheek, blending with the ocean spray that splashes my face. "I'm going to have to drop out of school. Figure out something else to do with my life."

His forehead wrinkles in confusion. "I'm lost, Ava. What are you talking about?"

"I transformed, Carter," I say. "Just like when you first turned me. I lost control."

"So, you just want to quit the human world?"

He makes me sound overly dramatic. Maybe I am. But damn it. I shouldn't be treading water right now. "What if it happens again?"

"You made it to the water, didn't you?"

"Yes, but—"

"But nothing. It happens. We manage."

"My mom doesn't get it," I say.

He frowns, pulling me even closer so that our chests touch, and I can feel his human form against me. "Is that what this is about? Of course she doesn't understand. She's still figuring things out like us."

"I'm ruining everything."

Sadness lines his blue-green eyes. He feels my emotions as much as I do, and with my sadness, I feel a tinge of guilt coming from Carter. It's been months since I've felt it. Not since getting to come home again.

"You are not, and you're putting too much pressure on yourself. Your parents will manage. The colonies will manage. Everything will be great. I promise," he says.

His words make me feel a teensy bit better. "How do you know?"

"Because I know how important everything is to you, and I know we'll make it work out. Everyone will talk about this forever. They'll say it was the best holiday, because you're with us now and you've given everyone so much." Carter brushes his lips against mine, kissing me sweetly, reminding me of how everyone is every time we're around. He's right. Things will work out regardless.

I sniffle. "You always know what to say to make me feel better, you know."

He kisses me once more. "I'm just glad I could."

Dipping under, I transform back into my human self without a problem. "I still can't believe I triggered a transformation. I'm so embarrassed. All I wanted was a hot shower with you and then to go get some tacos."

He laughs, pulling me with him to swim to shore. "I think I can make that happen."

At least one thing will go my way. I just hope everything else soon follows suit.

ALL OR NOTHING

"THANKS FOR DINNER, MATTY," I say, bumping my fist against his. "Never underestimate a mermaid's ability to eat before a two day swim next time."

He grabs my wrist and pulls me into a bear hug, rocking me back and forth. "I will beat you one of these days."

"Doubt it," Sapphire says, hugging me next.

"You're betting on Ava?" Matty holds his hand over his heart in fake shock.

"Damn right she is," Giselle says, fake punching Matty in

his arm.

Carter and Luna talk with Chloe, Daisy, and Logan in front of the door to the Taco Palace. Every few seconds, Carter glances at me, smiling, because he can feel the happiness I have in this moment. None of my friends care that I'm not traveling with them. None of them see Carter, or even Luna for that matter, as an outsider. They don't blame Carter for transforming me unlike my parents. My friends were all there when I went overboard. The ocean would've gotten me one way or another. But it let Carter save me so I could be who I am. I wouldn't change it. If only I could get my parents to understand. They can't just have the human part of me. It's all of me or nothing. I know they'd never want nothing.

An arm slides over my shoulders. "You all right, Aves?" Carter's question pulls me from my thoughts. So much for holding onto the happiness my friends bring when everything else is piling up in my mind.

I bob my head. "Just thinking about everything."

"Don't stress about it," he says. "It's going to be fine."

"He's right, Ava-babe," Logan says. My cheeks warm when I realize all my friends are looking at me. "I bet you twenty bucks it's going to be better than the Ocean Jewel."

"Yeah, plus, I'm sure Carter's still at your service," Daisy says, grinning.

I cover my face with my hands. "Shut up, you guys."

"Just please try not to exit the ocean naked all the time. I don't want Matty and Logan to think that just because you do it that it's cool if they do it, too. I've seen enough of their asses to last me the rest of my life." Chloe fake grimaces at all three guys. "No offense. Sort of."

I knew my friends wouldn't let Carter live tonight down. It's the first thing that came from Matty's mouth when we showed up for dinner. Just another naked in an awkward situation story I'm sure will be passed down for generations. At least it took my mind off the whole... *Don't think about it.*

"You just wait, Chloe. This is going to be a nude Christmas now. I think my suitcase might get lost at the airport," Logan says.

"Like you're that brave," Sapphire says, rolling her eyes.

"You think I won't do it?"

"Nope."

"Hundred bucks says I will." Logan holds out his hand.

Matty steps in and shakes it. "I'll take that bet."

"Damn it." Daisy smacks both guys on the backs of their heads. "I'll give you both a hundred bucks if you just stop while you're ahead."

"Deal," Matty and Logan say in unison.

Luna giggles from her place. She looks so cute in her deep blue sweater and black jeans with her long hair pulled into a ponytail. I'm so used to her in her kelp woven tops. "You are all so strange sometimes."

We all laugh.

"Don't even get them started," I say.

After saying goodbye to everyone, Giselle and Luna head to

Giselle's Mustang. Carter follows me to my BMW and opens the driver's side door for me. I get behind the wheel and start the engine but don't back out of the space.

My phone buzzes from my cup holder, and I see a call from my mom.

I groan without answering it.

"Want me to drive?" Carter asks. His concern sneaks into my mind, though I know he's trying to keep his emotions from me.

I shake my head. "I'm good."

"Want me to talk to your mom?" he asks.

I consider telling him yes. "No, let it go to voicemail."

My phone buzzes again. This time, a picture of Bailey and Wes pops up on the screen. I close my eyes for a second and then shift my car into reverse to back out of the space. Giselle and Luna already left the parking lot along with the rest of my friends.

When I reach the exit, I turn left instead of right to get to the freeway. Carter doesn't say anything as I navigate the familiar streets of Azure Waters and make my way to the private street of my beach community. It's rare that I drive here anymore, and I'm almost taken aback seeing the unfamiliar truck in the driveway—a gift from my parents to my sister when she got her permit. Basically returning from the dead was quite the surprise for the whole town, but my parents and their lawyers kept everything so private that there are a million rumors floating around about where Bailey's been all this time—pirates being my favorite—especially with the arrival of Wes by her side. All I know is that mermaids were definitely not part of the story Bailey and Wes came up with.

"You sure you don't want to just send a text?" Carter asks.

I rest my hands on the steering wheel. "I'm already not going to hear the end of this from everyone until January. Why did the full moon pick this year to fall on Winter Solstice? I bet your mom wouldn't make a big deal if it wasn't."

Carter smirks without saying a word.

"You're right. She would." I huff a breath. "Why can't things be normal?"

Carter links his fingers with mine and brings my hand to his lips to kiss my knuckles. "What's the fun in that? Think about it. Once everyone gets there, they'll be busy having too much fun to notice that things are different or they'll be busy experiencing new things—humans and merpeople alike. And when they are, we can sneak away and celebrate our own little holiday."

"Build a sandman instead of a snowman?" I ask.

He nods. "Hang shells instead of ornaments."

"Sand angels."

"The works."

Leaning across the center console to reach Carter, I brush my lips against his. His free hand slides into my hair, and we deepen our kiss. I could kiss him until morning if I knew my parents wouldn't come home to badger us with complaints. It takes a knock on the window to stop me from shifting from behind the wheel and onto Carter's lap in my parents' driveway.

I ease away and turn in my seat to meet Bailey's raised eyebrows. Wes stands in the doorway of the remodeled Victorian, silhouetted in the light glowing from the living room. After killing the engine, I swing my door open with Carter following my lead on the passenger's side, and I stand to face my sister.

"I thought you two might end up leaving if I didn't let you know I saw you pull up," Bailey says. "I wouldn't blame you, because I heard Mom complaining to Dad. Lucky for you, Mom went over to Anaya's and Dad went to work already."

"Must be an early Christmas miracle," I mutter. "Hopefully I didn't waste my only one."

Carter chuckles from next to me, and Bailey furrows her brows. She motions for us to follow her inside, and I drag my feet up the brick steps and into our warm living room. It hasn't changed much since I moved out, except my mom had a candid portrait of all of us framed and placed on the wall above the couch.

I stop in front of it, a smile crossing my face. It was taken at Celestiana Cove the one and only time I took humans there that weren't inhabitants. It's also where Mom and Dad met Carter's family. Everyone looks so happy, laughing and smiling. I can only hope the holiday can be half as good.

"...accidentally triggered a transformation." Carter's voice pulls my attention away from the photo.

I frown. "Carter, can we not announce that to the world?"

"I'm your sister, not the world, Avie. I know things haven't been all rainbows between us, but I do love you, and I want to be here for you. You don't have to be embarrassed for not being perfect. I'm sure the hell not." Bailey steps a few feet closer and hugs me. "I'm not exactly thrilled about an island Christmas, either."

I crinkle my nose. "Sorry about this."

"Hey, don't apologize. At least we'll be celebrating together, right? If it helps out, I'll think of a way to get Mom off your back."

"How will you do that?"

She smirks at Wes. "You'll see."

5

TIME TO CELEBRATE

I SHIVER ON THE BACK patio, staring at the moon hanging just above the horizon. We have two days to swim to Reefaria and another two there before we have to surface to meet my family at the Whitsunday Islands, where they've rented not only a beach mansion but also a private yacht for a few days to get the "best Great Barrier Reef experience." I'm pretty sure I can provide that myself without the luxury of a yacht, though I'm not going to say anything because this vacation feels like work already. Giselle's adventure will be my exception.

"You better surface and call me when you get there," Giselle says, standing on the sand next to me. She's an early riser and had even woken up before us to make breakfast. She never lets me leave on an ocean excursion of this magnitude without a goodbye. "I'll relay all messages to your mom. Bailey texted me and said she would handle everything else."

"Apparently she has some plan that'll distract my parents," I say.

She puffs air through her lips. "Good, because I don't know how much more I can say to get them to relax."

I laugh. "I owe you."

"Still hoping for a merman."

Luna kicks sand, bringing my attention to her. "I might have someone in mind."

Giselle claps. "Yes! Watch out Aves, Luna's going to replace you in the position of mermaid best friend. You might just be my part-time human BFF."

"Oh, I—" Luna's wide, sapphire eyes practically bulge from her head. "I'm not—"

"It's okay, Luna. Best friends aren't exclusive like mates. You're one of my best friends and so is Giselle." I turn to Giselle. "But they can also change."

Giselle fake glowers.

"I'm all set. Mom and Dad will be swimming straight to the Whitsundays in a few days." Carter exits the condo, adjusting the waterproof backpack on his shoulders. "I loaded our bags in your trunk, Gi."

"Great, thanks." Giselle gives Carter a hug. She turns toward me. "Remember, call me."

"Yes, Mother. Carter has the satellite phone and an extra battery." I give Giselle one last hug and watch her embrace Luna.

She opens the slider to our condo but just steps inside to watch us head to the waves. Carter twines his fingers with mine, pulling me through the sand and toward the lightening horizon. I brace myself for the freezing surf, knowing Carter won't let me ease in. He's a jump-in-and-get-it-over-with diver.

"This swim is going to be a little different, Aves. I can't carry both you and Luna the whole way so we're going to catch the currents to Reefaria to speed up travel time. Think you can handle it?" he asks, stopping on the shore.

A small wave washes over my bare feet, and I shiver from the cold water. "So, we're going to ride the EAC?"

He jerks his head to look at me. "You've been memorizing currents?"

I hold a straight face, because the only reason I know of the East Australian Current is from a movie. I consider lying and telling him yes, that I've learned a lot more from my freshman ocean lecture, but he'd see right through me.

I grin. "Come on, the EAC is kind of a big deal. I thought a movie about a clown fish searching for his son would've been your favorite movie as a merbabe. Bailey and I watched it all the time."

He snorts, bringing his hand up to cover his mouth. "I love

you, Aves. And yes, we'll take that current after hitting up the South Equatorial Current first." Oh, jeez. Turning into teacher mode. What have I started?

"There's a movie about currents?" Luna asks. "Can we watch it sometime?"

I laugh. "If you're okay knowing that the dad clownfish doesn't change sexes to take the place of the mom fish. There's one about a mermaid princess, too."

Before I can suck Luna into human television, Carter tugs us both forward. The freezing water stops the conversation as I release a squeal. My voice cuts off the second my head hits the swell, and I'm forced to dive. Carter unties my bikini bottoms for me before I have the chance, and seconds later I transform and inhale an icy breath of the sea. The water warms, my body adjusting. It helps that I can warm the water around us with ocean magic if I concentrate hard enough.

Carter slides his arms around me and pulls me in for a kiss. "There's no time to waste, my queen." He sends me some images of white sand beaches and crystalline waters with the thought.

Pulling away, I find Luna hovering in the sea next to us, her gold scales glittering in the early morning sunlight trickling from above. I reach out and grab her hand, and then Carter takes my other.

I only look back at the shores of La Tortuga Point once before we head out to sea.

The bright moon shines silver light across the rippling water. Luna sits on a rock next to me near some most-likely uninhabited island. I had no idea how many little islands there were throughout the ocean until transforming into a mermaid.

"So, when we first arrive, we'll need to sit down with the colony's elders. They'll appoint merpeople to perform certain tasks. Luckily, Reefaria is bigger than Pearlestria, so accommodating everyone won't be as big a task as it was there, and everyone opens their homes."

I nod, watching Carter's spark dart through the ocean not far from us. "What else should I know about?"

"My dad used to hold a huge feast before a sea lighting ceremony," she says, staring off in the distance. I don't have to feel her emotions to know that the thought ignites sadness in her. It's probably the first time she hasn't been with Attilonious for a holiday, and now I feel crappy as hell for switching things up so she won't be able to visit him at Celestiana Cove.

I pout my bottom lip. "I'm sorry, Luna."

She slaps her tail on the water hitting the rock. "What for?"

"You know, for asking you to be here instead of with your dad."

She grabs my hand. "Don't apologize. It's not like I can spend it with him under the full moon anyway. I'm where I'm supposed to be—with the rest of my pod. I'll see him after the solstice."

I bump my shoulder to hers. "You have no idea what you mean to me. I just hope I don't let you or anyone else down."

"You could never," she says. "Now stop worrying about it. This isn't a time for doubts. It's a time to celebrate what the ocean has given us—you included."

"You're right. I've never been more thankful."

6

REEFARIA

REEFARIA SPEAKS TRUE TO ITS name. In the Tasman Sea near New Zealand, the large merpeople colony teems with a different kind of beauty than the pearlescent rocks of Pearlestria. A series of interconnected reefs and rocks create the colony amid clear water that looks turquoise from the surface. Ocean magic flows through the sea, protecting this underwater paradise, shining with vibrant colors created by the ocean itself in the coral and sea plants. Bright reds and oranges among the greens of sea grass mimic a sunset in a meadow. Purple, pink, and blue sea anemones speckle the enormous reef like underwater flowers, and a herd of seahorses swim from their home among the sea life to greet me.

I laugh out loud, sending a stream of bubbles through the water. I can't help it. Getting so close and personal with the creatures around me is one of my favorite things. Carter knows better than to mess with anything that comes within my reach these days, regardless if a fish looks good enough to eat for him. Of course, he'd never hurt a seahorse.

"Queen Ava, welcome back to Reefaria." A muscular merman with long blond hair and a copper tail swims in front of me, shooing away all my new seahorse friends. He grabs my hands, pulling me close, and kisses both my cheeks. "It was quite the surprise to discover the desire for a Summer Solstice here with the full moon falling on the longest night in the Northern Hemisphere."

I force myself to smile despite hearing the confusion, even disappointment, in his thought to me. I don't really want to say it's because my human family was behind my decision, because I don't want the colonies to feel like I put humans before them, so I say, "I hope it's not too much trouble, Sun."

"Of course not. We're thrilled to host things here. I have selected a few merpeople to assist you with whatever you need," Sun says.

Sun was a young advisor to the former king, and named because of the color of his hair as a merbabe, according to a memory he shared with me on my first visit to Reefaria over the summer. The language of the merpeople varies between images and words, and many speak multiple human languages on land because of how merpeople teach each other through memories. Once a memory is shared, it stays with you. It's why bonds and community are so important. Merpeople live life as one entity.

"Actually, they'll be helping Princess Luna. Carter and I will be taking orders from her on everything," I say, pulling away to motion to Luna and Carter, floating behind me.

Sun frowns for a split second, surprising me. He's too close to me that thankfully no one else notices. I knew things would be different now that Attilonious' merman essence was taken back by the ocean, but I didn't realize that some attitudes would've shifted with Luna. I just hope she doesn't notice or care. She has enough to worry about already.

"Perfect, my queen." He turns his attention to Luna. "Thank you for coming, princess."

"Of course, Sun," Luna says, reaching out to touch the merman's hand.

He smiles. "Now, you must all be tired from your journey. How about I catch something for you to eat while you rest? The royal reef awaits. If you need something, please ask Sandy. He's posted outside your home."

Carter swims closer. "That sounds great, thank you."

With a small nod and a flick of his tail, Sun swims through a tunnel in the reef wall and disappears. Carter adjusts the bag on his shoulder, and Luna twists her lips, staring in the direction that Sun left in.

I sling my arm over Luna's shoulder. "I have to surface real quick to call Giselle. Want to come?"

She presses her lips into a line and then shakes her head. "That's okay. I'm going to swim around the colony to get a sense of things. Meet you at the royal reef when you're done?"

I glance to Carter. "Sure. We won't be long."

We wait until Luna swims away before Carter flips me onto his back and jets off. Instead of heading straight to the surface, he navigates through the colorful, lively reef until we hit open water. The shallows sneak up faster than I expect them to, and it's then that I realize that Reefaria isn't far from an island.

Carter slides us right onto the beach, digging his hands in the soft sand to keep himself propped up as a wave slides over our tails. I roll off his back, tilting my head toward the sky. It's been months since I've been directly on shore in my mermaid form. I forgot how much I love it.

The bright sunlight sparkles over my cerulean scales, the same color as the cloudless sky, and I spit water at Carter. He laughs, his voice catching on the salty breeze of the desolate yet breathtaking beach.

Flipping onto his back, he lies next to me, letting the balmy air dry the sand sticking to his tan skin. "What do you think?"

I draw hearts in the sand at my side. "Do you have a map of the world with all the secret uninhabited places to take me to memorized or something that you don't share with me?"

He chuckles. "So, do you like it?"

"It's amazing." I lace my fingers with his. "And I still want to know how you know."

"I asked Sun," he says, sitting up. He slings the waterproof bag off his shoulders. "There are a few of them we can check out, you know. If you want to sleep under the stars."

My cheeks flush, warmth traveling from the tip of my tail to my chest, sending my heart beating wildly. Carter pulls me in for a kiss, trailing his lips away from mine to brush down my jawline to the bikini strap on my shoulder. He nudges it off and kisses my clavicle. His hands move from mine and slide along the ridge that separates my tail from my stomach. He lifts me onto his lap from the back of my tail, and I run my hands over his sun-kissed shoulders, dusting sand from him as I do.

"Carter," I whisper. "You're going to make me not want to go back to Reefaria if you continue doing what you're doing."

His warm breath tickles my skin. "This may have been my plan all along. Make everyone think we were obligated to be here so I could keep you all to myself before the craziness starts."

I tilt my head back to stare into his jewel-like eyes, even more brilliant in the sunlight. His dimples peek on his scruffy face as he smiles the smile he saves just for me. And I realize he's completely serious.

"Carter, I—"

He interrupts me with a kiss. "I've already discussed it with Luna, and she agreed with me that this was best."

I scrunch my face. "Best? I need to be there for the colonies."

He sighs. "You will be. But I need you to not be so stressed out that you accidentally start transforming again, and obviously the pressure is getting to you. You don't need your sea stone ring to transform, so I can't ask you to take it off so you don't turn into a human if the advisors start sharing their dissatisfaction with you because things aren't identical to all the other solstices under Attilonious."

"If I do, then I'll change back. I'm not a newbie anymore, and it's not like we're staying at a landlocked hotel." I turn away to stare at the ocean. I know he and Luna had good intentions, but the solstice is my responsibility. Why should Luna have to take up my slack? That's not fair.

Carter gently pinches my chin, forcing me to look at him. "You're really going to argue about spending a few days with me in paradise, Aves?"

As much as I want to give in to that delicious pout of his, I can't enjoy myself knowing that Luna's going to be working her tail off on something that is my fault to begin with. My love of the land shouldn't ruin things in the sea for everyone else.

I suck in my top lip for a second. "It doesn't feel right. We really should help."

"You know Attilonious never did, right? No one would even think twice."

"I'm not Attilonious, Carter," I say.

"Point taken, Aves," he says, leaning in to kiss my forehead. "But we're coming back here tonight. I wasn't kidding about sleeping under the stars."

I smile. "Only if we get a lot done."

He hands me the waterproof bag. "Then hurry and call Giselle. There's no more time to lose."

ROYAL DUTIES

"NOTHING SAYS THE HOLIDAYS MORE than gathering a feast to savagely devour until you sink to the ocean floor," I say, peering at a school of fish collected by the colony's hunters—cod, salmon, flounder, mackerel, even a few eels—that have been corralled in the center of the colony. They're not netted or trapped or anything, but they're not swimming for their little fishy lives either. The only time they wander from their hand-selected school is to swim closer to me.

Reaching out, I send a small current toward the ugliest fish

I've seen here. Its big eyes protrude from its head, and it has a green-tinted, almost pointed oval body with spiky dorsal fins that lead to a silly, tiny tail that almost looks like a miniature feather duster. Definitely something I won't eat, though I probably won't be taking a bite out of any of the selection.

"That's an Oreo Dory," Carter says from next to me. "You might like it. It's mild tasting."

I grimace. "It's hideous."

"Not like you eat the cute ones, either." He pokes me in the side, a smirk playing on his lips. "One of these days, I'm going to wear you down, and you'll just give in to your mermaid instincts and—"

"Want to bet on it?" I ask, raising an eyebrow.

"And give you a reason to be stubborn? No thanks."

I laugh, a stream of bubbles trailing from my mouth and toward the surface. Carter slides his arm around my waist and hugs me from the side. He flicks his tail, swimming us away from the fish set for the feast before I can do anything rash like send them on their merry way with a special royal pardon from me.

Luna hovers in the center of a large sand channel with rock and coral houses on either side not unlike the sand channel in Pearlestria. Her gold tail sweeps the sand back and forth, creating a cloud around her. She watches a few merpeople move a slab of rock, setting it down in the center. It probably weighs a ton, but weight doesn't stop merpeople. I've seen Carter lift boulders underwater. The merpeople drop the platform, sending a cloud of sand our way.

I squint through the haze. "What's the platform for?"

Luna places her hands on her hips. "The moonlight ceremony. This should give you a view of the entire colony." In Pearlestria, I'd have done the ceremony outside the castle, which sits in the center. Here, there's nothing really. The royal reef is at the far north section connected to the barrier wall.

"Oh." I glance at Carter who shrugs.

Merpeople love their ceremonies. Me? Not so much. It's a lot of pressure. Worse than finals week. I can't just memorize what I'm supposed to say and rush through it like a presentation. I must truly believe in the words, gather ocean magic, and be the mermaid everyone expects me to be—which is nothing short of perfect. I'm not a ruler, but the colonies still rely on me to lead. Lead them how? I'm still figuring it all out.

"This is why you should let me handle all the little things, Ava. You have enough to think about. The speech my dad gave every solstice won't work for you. You must call upon the ocean to guide you through this, not hang around and help me decorate." Luna motions for her team of merpeople to move the platform over a few feet. Carter swims forward to help them. "I have all this under control despite what I hear the elders say."

Taking her hand, I pull her back even though no one can hear our private conversation, even Carter. Not when I project my thoughts just to Luna.

"What are you talking about? They're talking about us?"

Luna's long, black tresses swirl through the water, veiling

her from me. "Not us. Just me. But I don't want you to worry about it. It's nothing, really."

I wave her hair out of the way to look at her. "Doesn't sound like nothing."

She shrugs. "I don't know if you're aware of this, but merpeople love to talk, and ever since..." Her thoughts trail off. "Let's just say that some merpeople question why I still frequently visit my dad. It makes them question my loyalty to you."

"Why wouldn't you visit him? He's your dad. He's family."

"They don't see it like that. The ocean shunned him because he's unworthy, which means I should disown him, too. They also believe I shouldn't still have a royal position." She keeps her expression emotionless as she tells me.

"Well, if they have a problem, they can take it up with me. I chose you as my advisor, and you will be my advisor until you tell me you wish to no longer be," I say.

She nods, a small smile on her lips. "I know. It's why I didn't want to say anything. I can handle myself."

"But you don't have to hide things to try to protect me. I care about you and your feelings. And you and Carter need to stop treating me like I'm a transformation away from disaster."

Her giggle tinkles through my mind. "I don't think that, but I do still think you need to prepare."

My shoulders slump. "Fine, but you better let me help with my ceremony top. I can't get stuck with all the boring stuff."

"We'll make a night of it."

"Good."

The bright moon hangs in the black sky directly overhead, sparkling off the rippling surface. Though I don't need air to breathe in my mermaid form, staying near the ocean's floor started making me feel suffocated. I don't know if it's that more and more merpeople arrive by the hour and insist on greeting me or the fact that I still have no idea what to say during the moonlight ceremony just days away, but something draws me to the air to just breathe.

I cup a handful of water in my palm, concentrating on freezing it so it doesn't slip through my fingers. Silver moonbeams catch off the still surface, and I glance at my mermaid reflection. My cerulean eyes, the same color of my scales, shine from within this form that I still have trouble accepting as my own. Even though I feel like me and can see my tail, feel the power of my swim, the warmth of the spark in my chest, seeing my eyes always throws me off. Because I'm Queen Ava, human-born, warrior-bonded, ocean-blessed liaison between the land and the sea and not Ava Adair from Azure Waters, college student, dating a surf instructor while living with her best friend, the girl the surface world knows me to be.

I lower my hand, suspending the now glowing orb of sea water in front of me. Gathering more water into my palm, I create a few more glowing orbs under the moonlight until it looks like I've reached into the midnight sky and plucked the burning stars from the sky to bring them to earth.

"You know, you used to be annoying and confusing, but a whole lot better at guiding me." My voice echoes through the air, bouncing off the still surface. I'm not exactly sure if the ocean can hear me, but if I put the words out there, maybe it'll be enough to get me through this crazy holiday for both my land and water families. "Am I wrong to change tradition?"

A swell rises from the calm sea and splashes me in the face. Carter breaks the surface in front of me, and I sigh. Of course the ocean wasn't going to respond. I lose concentration, and the moonlit water orbs splash back into the sea.

"We're basically done here. Luna really knows how to prepare a celebration efficiently," he says.

I pat the water with my hand. "You sure?"

"Positive, Aves. I mapped out the great swim for you, and we can work on the ceremonial stuff anywhere. I also might have just the place to do it."

Turning my gaze to his, I can't help smiling at his mischievous smirk. "What are you planning?"

"Can't your mate surprise you?"

I shrug. "Only with good surprises."

This gets a laugh out of him. His deep voice hums through the air, wrapping around me in such joy that my heart picks up pace. He grins wider, the blinking spark in his own chest matching my own.

"I think I can manage that."

"You think the merpeople will go for it?" I ask.

After a quick swim around Reefaria to say goodbye to the residents and new arrivals, Luna basically shooed us away like I shoo away overly playful animals like dolphins and seals when they want to turn me into their sole entertainment back in La Tortuga Point. I extended an offer for Luna to join us, but she said she had a few things to finish before she heads to the Whitsundays on her own tomorrow night.

"I love the idea, Aves. Seriously. Pretty sure this is going to be the best solstice I've ever had. And Christmas. You don't even know how excited I am to experience it. I've only ever seen stuff on TV. I've never actually been on land for that day since my parents always treated the Winter Solstice as a vacation to the colonies to spend time with our family." Carter links his hands around my wrist to slide me up farther on his back until I rest my chin on the crook between his shoulder and neck.

I kiss just below his ear. "Your excitement makes me nervous. I don't want you to be disappointed. We usually just exchange gifts, stuff our faces, and watch every holiday movie we can squeeze in. Nothing like how Winter Solstice is celebrated."

"Still sounds amazing, Ava."

"You're ridiculous."

"If you knew why, you wouldn't think so." His thoughts take on a new seriousness, and he slows down to flip me off his back and into his arms so I have to face him.

"I was only kidding about you being ridiculous. You don't have to explain anything to me," I say, leaning forward to give him a soft kiss. I pull his bottom lip between mine while trailing my hands down his chest to cover the spark that flashes in rhythm with mine.

"But I want to, because I never thought I'd ever get such a life with you, Aves. Even though I've spent the majority of my life on land, I always thought if I fell in love with a human, that we'd follow tradition like every human-born turned mermaid had, that I'd be the one showing you my world, and we'd make it our world," he says.

I can't stop the smile forming on my lips, interrupting our kiss. "I love our world."

"You haven't always," he reminds me. "It's always been you giving up things for my life, my existence, to be my mate, and a part of my family."

I cup his face and stare at him. His turquoise jewel eyes hold me in such intensity that I can feel the warmth from my spark blossoming up my neck and into my cheeks. "That's not true. You gave things up for me."

"Not the same."

I inhale the warm water. Carter's always held onto guilt for my transformation. "But things are great now. I don't want you holding onto all of that anymore. You shouldn't feel guilty for choosing me."

He rests his forehead on mine. "I don't, promise. Especially because we changed things. And it's the change that makes me so—" He pauses, gathering his thoughts. "I'm just so happy I get a part of you I never expected or knew I wanted. I'm part of your family now instead of you just being a part of mine. We're living life how you wanted—we wanted. I get to know the girl you were before you met me, which reminds me how lucky I am every day that you love me. I get to share the life I thought I stole from you that you had no choice but to give up, and not only that, but you did it for me. So, call me ridiculous for being excited for the little things like celebrating a holiday with your family. I'll own it."

It's rare that Carter leaves me speechless, but I'm definitely speechless—and breathless, and whoa. I just stare at him, my mind a complete mess.

He smirks at me, flashing his dimples.

"I—" I still can't find my words, so I kiss him, sending image after image of the little memories from my life I never think to share. Like the first Christmas after Bailey was swept away on a rip current when my parents rented a cabin in Big Bear to get away because staying home was too hard. And another Christmas where we all spent the night at Sapphire and Giselle's grandmother's in New York.

I share with him every Christmas I can remember. The year of the turkey fiasco where my mom, Anaya, and Ruby drank too many mimosas and forgot they were the ones cooking. Another year from when I was little where Bailey and I had matching elf pajamas, and she hated that our parents made us dress like twins. Every memory I share makes me smile wider and wider, because they tell a story about my human life. Things I had forgotten about.

Carter pulls away, his eyes still closed as he lives through the memories I share as if they're his own. After a long moment, he gives me a strange look, his lips half smiling, his eyes narrowed in what I can only describe as determination. Pulling me close again, he holds me against him and takes off at a speed so fast I lose all sense of direction. Everything's just a blur as we swim by.

Carter doesn't stop swimming until morning sunlight trickles into the water from overhead, and we transform into our human selves in the shallows of what I assume are the Whitsunday Islands.

I break the surface and spit out seawater. "You know, my family isn't going to be here yet. I thought we could explore the Great Barrier Reef or something."

Carter shakes his head. "We'll have plenty of time to do that when they do come."

"So, what's the plan?"

"I may have called your parents and had them arrange something early for us," he says, smiling.

"Seriously?" I practically drag him through the waves to the shore.

"You're going to love it," he says. "Maybe this can be our tradition."

I hug him in the surf. "I love that. *Our* tradition."

8

NEW TRADITIONS

"IT'S LIKE A GLASS HOUSE," Carter says, peering through the floor-to-ceiling window in the living room of one of the two beach houses my parents and their friends rented to accommodate everyone. The view of the beach is breathtaking with the blue waters stretching out endlessly.

"My parents did say it had a great view." I slide open the glass door to the deck overlooking the infinity pool on the story below where five bedrooms are located just for us kids. All our parents are staying in the just as—if not more—luxurious house through the gate next door. "But you know, it just doesn't feel like Christmas to me."

Carter comes up behind me and rests his chin on my shoulder. "Just wait. You haven't seen the whole house yet. I plan to change your mind."

Pulling me back inside, he guides me through the living room to an opaque glass wall that slides open from the center to connect the main living area to a huge entertainment room with a projector screen setup, cozy couches to relax on, a selection of swimming gear with what looks like a dozen wetsuits, and a huge fake Christmas tree in the corner.

"I guess real trees are hard to come by here," I say, running my fingers over the plastic needles of the tree that will need a ladder to decorate.

Footsteps sound from behind us, tapping across the shiny wood floors. The property manager, Ms. Tonkin, carries a few bags on her arms. "What do ya think? The Glass Estate is a beaut, isn't it?"

Carter takes the bags from her to set on one of the game tables. "Perfect, Ms. Tonkin. This is exactly what I had in mind. Thanks." He moves the bags with a smile before I can see what's in them. Sneaky merman.

"Oh, don't mention it. And call me Whitney, will ya?" She peers around the room with a smile.

I offer my hand out. "Of course. Thank you again. Everything is exactly like my parents described."

"Great. You can find my number on the icebox if ya need

anything else." She nods with another smile and starts to turn to leave, but stops. "Oh, and watch out for stingers. I'd wear the stinger suits so ya don't ruin your holiday with a trip to the hospital."

"Definitely don't want that to happen," Carter says, smirking at me.

Whitney leaves us alone, and I turn to Carter. "Stingers?"

"Jellyfish," he says. "Remember the bloom we passed on our way in?"

"Guess I'll be swimming the area to shoo them all away for everyone. I'm not going to spend any time at the hospital with my friends if they get stung."

Carter digs through the bags without looking at me. "Good thing you won't have to with my mom around. I'm sure she can tend to stings without needing to seek medical attention. You probably could do it, too. Just ask her about it if you're worried."

Always nice to have a mermaid healer on hand, I suppose. "I'll just give the jelly—stingers—a stern talking to."

"Hey, the animals might start talking back to you one of these days." He peeks up from the bag, trying not to smile.

I fake glare. "You're just jealous that they love me more than you."

"Because you're as threatening as a guppy, Aves. They know you won't eat them." He laughs at his own teasing, making me laugh. He might have a point. I'm probably the only mermaid in existence that refuses to hunt and catch a fish before devouring it in the freshest form of sushi.

"Do I need to remind you that I can probably sink this island?"

"But you won't."

I step closer and slide my arms around him. He shifts the bags away from me before I can look in them. "What're you hiding?"

He chuckles again, turning away. As I reach to snatch one of the bags from him, he plops a red Santa hat on my head, a huge smile crossing his face. He adjusts one on his own head, and I can't remember a time where I've seen him this excited—not normal excited but giddy, child-like excitement that only comes with believing in Christmas magic.

"What is all this?" I ask.

"I saw how pouty you were in Reefaria that Luna wasn't letting you help with the decorations, so I made sure you'd be in charge of it here...unless I messed up and you want me to call Whitney to have someone do it like was planned."

I shake my head, my hair slapping my cheeks. "We're definitely decorating. And then after, I want to go to the store and get some baking supplies."

He kisses me, sending me an image of me wearing my favorite pineapple print apron over a bikini top and shorts. My hair is piled on my head in a messy bun, and I'm smiling with a glob of frosting I purposely put on my bottom lip.

I laugh, my neck burning with the memory. "I'm pretty sure I wasn't as sexy as you remember."

"Doubt it, Aves." He lifts me into his arms, kissing me again, holding me so close that all thoughts of baking and decorating leave my mind.

All I can think about is Carter and our room with the view. "I think the decorating and baking can wait," I whisper.

He strolls toward the staircase leading to the bedrooms. "I think so, too."

The scent of sugar and gingerbread cookies wafts through the air. I have both recipes, belonging to my grandma, memorized because I've been in charge of the Christmas cookies since I was twelve. Carter doesn't think I notice him eating a cookie every time I turn my back, but I let him without saying anything because of how brightly he smiles when I glance at him. His joy and excitement hits me in waves. He can barely contain himself now that the sun has set and rainbow Christmas lights sparkle from every place Carter could put them.

"I don't know what kind of cake you're making, but I can't wait to try it," he says, stealing a few blueberries from the towel I laid out some fresh, cut up fruit on.

"It's called Pavlova," I say, arranging the berries and sliced kiwis on top of the whipped cream frosting to look like a tree with ornaments. "And you can't taste it yet. I made it for everyone."

He pouts, making me laugh. "But it looks so good. I love meringue anything."

Kissing his sweet lips, I taste the butter cream frosting I

used to decorate the sugar cookies. I brush my tongue over his, sending him the memory of his failed attempt to be sneaky, and he chuckles against my lips.

"You caught me," he says.

"Those ones were for you anyway. I already put the ones for everyone away."

"And you think *I'm* sneaky," he says.

Pulling myself away from Carter, I turn back to the counter to put the Pavlova into a container. Carter helps me clean up while simultaneously making a mess from cookie crumbs. I throw a hand towel at him, and he charges me and tosses me over his shoulder. He doesn't put me down until we're standing at the edge of the pool lit in moonlight.

"You don't want to go to the beach to swim?" I ask, wiggling from his arms so I can dip my bare foot in the cool, chlorinated water.

"Nope. We'll have plenty of time fo—"

The chime of the doorbell echoes from a speaker on the wall near the slider, cutting off his words. I frown, glancing at Carter since it's late. "Are you expecting someone?"

He presses his lips together and shakes his head. "No, but I'll send them away. Wait here."

The doorbell rings again two more times in quick successions. Carter kisses my cheek and strolls back inside to answer it. I sit down on the non-slip concrete and dip my legs into the pool while I wait. The almost full moon reflects off the still mirror-like surface.

Voices drift through the air, and I lean closer to the open door to try to hear them.

"What do you mean everyone's here?" Carter's voice rises over the quiet night. "They knew we'd be back in a couple days."

"I tried to reason with them, but they wanted to be near Ava. You know how the colonies feel about her and how important the solstice is." It's Luna. "I couldn't stop them."

"Well, tell them to go back. We have nothing prepared for anyone to come to land here." Carter sounds more annoyed by the second. I know if I don't get up soon, he might unintentionally yell at Luna for something that sounds like it's not in her control.

"They've already picked one of the uninhabited islands nearby, but a few have come to shore here and are waiting on the beach."

"Seriously? Here?"

"You know how we get near a full moon. The excitement of the holiday doesn't help the matter. I don't know what else to do. Everything was fine until you left. It's like Ava embodies the call of the sea. You can't feel it because she's always with you. I just thought I always missed her because she's my friend."

While Luna's words give me a warm and fuzzy feeling, they kind of freak me out. Not because she misses me—I miss her, too—but the fact that she equated me to the call of the sea, which I find quite uncomfortable on the full moon if I resist too long to return to the ocean.

Puffing out a breath through my lips, I push to my feet. I know Carter will try to send her away to deal with things because neither of us are used to the position bestowed on us.

I step inside and cold air from the AC sends goosebumps over my skin. Carter and Luna stand in the entryway at the top of the stairs. I was right about Carter being annoyed. He rocks on his heels, his hands laced behind his head. Luna shifts on her bare feet with her arms crossed over a damp sundress, her black hair dripping saltwater on the tile. They both turn to look at me.

Carter forces a smile while Luna frowns.

"What's going on?" I ask.

"Nothing," the two of them say in unison.

"I heard your conversation, and it doesn't sound like nothing," I quip, raising an eyebrow.

"Luna just needed some advice on—"

"It's fine, Carter. Everything can wait until morning. I'll figure it out," Luna says, cutting him off.

It's my turn to frown. "Luna."

"Really, Ava. I can do this. I shouldn't have come here tonight. I know how much you need to focus on your duties and—"

"Duties? We were about to go swimming in the pool. It's okay, really. If there are some unexpected visitors hanging around, I want to talk to them. I can't have a bunch of naked people strolling the beach outside of the house when my family arrives."

"We could pretend that your parents overlooked the fine print about a nude beach," Carter says. "You know, I wouldn't mind participating with you, Aves."

I blush, playfully slapping his arm. "You are so not helping."

He flashes his dimples, trying to hide his smile. "I thought it was a solid plan."

Luna glances between us. "I should get back to the beach. Sorry I bothered you two."

She spins on her feet and rushes out the front door before I have a chance to even say anything. Carter shrugs, and I narrow my eyes at him, all the flirty banter now gone. Without saying anything to Carter, I jog out the door after Luna, practically full-on sprinting to catch up to her.

"Luna, wait. Let me help," I say, reaching out to grab her shoulder.

Her glassy eyes shine in the moonlight. "I'm failing at my duties, and I don't know how to fix things."

"You're failing? No way. I'm the one who is failing. I should've never let Carter convince me to leave. I shouldn't have let my family guilt me into coming here for that matter. They know I live a different life now. They should've asked. It's just hard balancing both worlds." Tears rim my own eyes from seeing how distraught Luna is, and I feel like utter crap.

Luna places her hand on my shoulder. "You're doing a great job, Ava. If you weren't, merpeople wouldn't be standing on the beach at all right now."

I groan. "But the fact that I wish they weren't proves I suck."

Luna pouts. "At least they'll listen to you. I'm starting to feel like an outcast in the ocean. I hate to say it, but I kind of want to run back inside and lock the door."

I glance over my shoulder at the beach. "Do it. You deserve to escape after everything you've done for us. If staying on land is what you want, do it."

Since the day I met Luna in Pearlestria I've known how much she wanted to escape the waves and go to land. But after her father lost his fins, she decided to remain in Pearlestria to help out with the transition of power to me. We both split our time, but I live on land while she lives in the sea. But now, standing under the moonlight with her, hearing her desires, I'm pretty sure she doesn't want to remain in the sea.

And if she doesn't, I don't want her to, even if it means more ocean time for me. I'll manage. I have to. This is what I was chosen to do. Unite the land and sea, and bringing Luna to land full time will help. And not just at Celestiana Cove. She'd thrive in the human world.

She blinks the tears from her eyes. "Really?"

I nod. "Yeah, really. I also think you should leave Pearlestria to come to shore permanently."

"I agree with Ava." I didn't even hear Carter come up behind us. "You can take our room in the condo."

I spin to face him. "What?"

He smirks. "I've been talking with Giselle."

A mixture of emotions rushes through me. Surprise, annoyance, a tiny bit of anger—this is something to talk about with me before just giving our room to Luna. The fact that Carter and Giselle talked without me kind of drives me a little crazy. "Well, you should've been talking about it with *me.*"

"Aves—"

I raise my hand up. "You know what? Why don't you take Luna back to the house and get her set up. I'll handle the merpeople."

Without saying another word, I straighten my shoulders and strut toward the beach. So much for a merry Christmas for me.

9

IMPORTANCE OF UNITY

A FEW SILHOUETTES STAND ON the beach not far from the walking path that took me to it from the front door. The almost full moon glitters on the surface of the ocean in a silver path, and I spot a few dozen flickering lights within the waves as more merpeople wait offshore.

"What are you all doing here?" I ask, strolling into the soft beach sand.

A familiar mermaid with blue streaked hair turns to face me in the sand. Luckily, she's wearing a swimsuit, and I notice the others with her are also dressed.

Grandmer, Starla's mom and Carter's grandma, offers me a warm smile. "Joining you for the solstice of course."

I frown. "But we're celebrating in Reefaria on the full moon."

"Oh, Ava. Can you not feel the excitement in the sea? Surely you understand how difficult it is on the colonies to know that you're spending the next few days on land."

"Yeah, but—"

"We promise not to be a bother. The elders agreed it would be fine to emerge on one of the uninhabited islands nearby until you could join us. We want to celebrate the solstice and the human holiday this year." The sparkle of joy in Grandmer's eyes makes it incredibly hard to get upset. She sounds just as excited as Carter.

I relax my shoulders. How am I supposed to deny the merpeople the chance to experience the human world with me? I've talked about the importance of uniting the land and sea for months, and this is my opportunity to grow.

"You know what? I think it's a great idea. But I need time to prepare. There isn't enough room for everyone here, so we'll have to figure things out. But tomorrow, okay?"

Grandmer smiles. "I'll inform the others if you'd like."

I nod. "Thank you."

Hugging Grandmer once, I motion to the small group of merpeople to head back to the waves. I wait on the sand and watch the ocean until all of the blinking lights disappear.

"Ava." Carter stands on the cement path without stepping into the sand. I turn away from the water to glance at him. "You're an amazing leader. You could have ordered everyone back to Reefaria to wait for the solstice, you know? They'd have listened."

I kick my foot through the powdery sand. "I could never."

"That's why you're the perfect queen."

With the way he looks at me, a soft smile spreading across his face and the moonlight reflecting in his eyes, I know he means every word. He also makes it incredibly hard to be mad at him for offering Luna our room without even talking to me.

"Are you trying to sweet talk your way out of trouble?" I ask, remaining just out of reach of the waves.

Carter steps forward, closing the distance, and wraps his arms around me. "You bet I am. Is it working? Because the last thing I want is for you to be upset on what is supposed to be a perfect vacation."

I sigh. "You know why I'm upset, right?"

"Yes, and I'm sorry. I wasn't thinking. I had assumed you'd be okay with it since we've talked about getting a place of our own before," he says.

"When we could afford it," I argue. "You can't expect my parents to pay for another place, and after almost transforming out of water the other night, I don't want to attempt to live anywhere away from the bea—"

He cuts me off with a kiss. He slowly pulls away, making sure I'm not going to continue to argue. "We will live on the beach, without your parents help, because I've been given a crazy awesome opportunity."

I crinkle my eyebrows. "What are you talking about?"

He smiles. "I was going to wait until solstice to give you this, but you're already so stressed about everything that I can't wait." Carter pulls a tiny bag from the pocket of his shorts and holds it up to me.

"What is it?" I ask.

"Just open it."

Smiling, I dig my fingers into the palm-sized bag, half expecting a piece of jewelry, but instead pull out a set of keys and a card. Not just any card. A business card with the Big Swell Surf School and Shop logo on it, along with Carter's name and the word *owner* underneath it.

My mouth drops open. "What is this?"

"One is the key to our new store and the other is for the apartment above it," he says.

I can barely form any words, so I do the only thing I can think of. I fling my arms around Carter and kiss him, letting him pick me off my feet to spin me around. Owning a watersports store was his dream before he turned me into a mermaid, and even then, I knew it was his goal, following in his dad's footsteps. And I can't believe it's happening.

"How? When?" I ask. I knew Travis hired Carter because he had planned to retire soon, but I didn't know he was planning to sell the store.

"Remember when my mom happened to show up at our

house at five in the morning?" he asks.

I raise an eyebrow.

"She happened to already be in town with my dad. They bought the store and will sign it over to me when we repay them."

"You guys are so sneaky," I say. "And I'm so happy for you."

"For us," he says.

"For us."

"These are definitely coming home with us," I say, tracing my fingers over the long strands of colorful sea glass Luna spent all morning threading through fishing line to add to our tree.

Carter helps me wrap them around the fake Christmas tree, giving it the perfect beachy touch for our summer holiday. He even managed to find a fake sea star to wire to the top. The only thing that would make the tree even more perfect is if we hauled it outside and stuck it into the sand.

"Think Giselle would be okay with year-round decorations?" Carter asks.

I smirk. "I don't know, but it won't matter in a few weeks, right?"

He kisses my cheek. "Right."

Luna adjusts a few more mermaid made ornaments and steps back to look at our creation. "It's beautiful. The perfect blend of the land and sea."

The doorbell rings, sending a musical chime through the

air. Glancing once more at the tree, I head to the foyer and spot two figures through the glass window before I have a chance to peer through the peephole.

Starla and Mateo stand on the porch still dripping with ocean water. I don't have a chance to step back before Carter's dad scoops me into a bear hug, swinging me back and forth, getting the front of my sundress wet.

"You two are early," I say, straightening my dress when Mateo puts me back on my feet.

"We were just so excited," Mateo says, glancing at Starla.

"Kind of like the rest of the colonies," Carter says, coming up next to me. He hands his parents each a towel to dry off.

Luna pops in from the living room. "Speaking of the colonies, want me to go check on them?"

Carter and I both crinkle our noses at each other and then laugh.

He slides his arm over my shoulders. "We can handle it."

"We'll come with," Starla says. "I haven't been to Reefaria in forever."

I purse my lips. "Actually, the col—"

"We've decided to switch things up again," Carter says, cutting me off. "There are a dozen uninhabited islands around, so everyone decided to come to land until solstice."

"What?" Starla asks.

Luna clears her throat. "It's my fau—"

I shake my head at her. There's no way I'm going to let her carry any ounce of guilt for something that was out of her control. "It's going to be great starting some new traditions. Just wait until you see our tree. If you want, you can stay here and rest. Carter and I won't be long."

Starla looks at Mateo, who smiles at her like he's happy to hang out anywhere as long as it's with her. It's the same look Carter gives me. "Well, I—"

"Ava made all sorts of desserts," Carter says, speaking up.

"We'll wait here," Mateo says.

I turn to Luna. "Why don't you stay here and show them around? Maybe the three of you can go shopping for a few things. I have some money in my purse for you, Luna. A thank you for all your hard work."

"Oh, Ava, you know I don't need—"

"Just take it," I say, hugging her. "And don't get too used to Australian currency. It's different compared to back home— this is way prettier."

Her eyes widen. "Really? Humans just make everything so complicated. How will I ever survive on land?"

"Princess Luna is leaving Pearlestria?" Starla asks.

I nod. "Now's the perfect time to transition with my break from school. I'll make the announcement on the solstice and appoint someone to take her place."

Starla grins. "Oh, princess, how wonderful! I'll never forget permanently moving onto land. I was your age, too." If only she were this excited when Carter told her we'd be living on land. Of course now, times have changed. Even in the last few months. I'm sure she's happy for us now.

Carter pulls me away from his parents and Luna when his mom starts droning on about everything there is to know about the land, like I haven't already showed or told Luna before.

The balmy morning air blows strands of my blond hair from my face, and I stroll down the pathway that leads to the waves. The bright sunshine beams overhead, and I stop the second I hit the sand and tilt my head up. It's strange feeling this warm, knowing that it's supposed to be cold. I should be wearing a sweater and jacket instead of my sundress and bikini.

I peer around the beach, the closest beach-goer a good distance away, and then drag Carter into the water, allowing it to soak the hem of my dress. He shrugs out of his T-shirt and tosses it to the sand. I kiss him as he helps me untie the halter straps of my dress. I dive into a wave the second it's off my head, leaving Carter in the waist deep waves.

It only takes him a few seconds to wrap his hands around my waist. We transform together, holding hands, and I allow the tropical sea into my lungs, pushing water out through my gills. My cerulean scales glitter in the sunlight trickling down to me in glowing streaks from the surface. Carter greets me with another kiss, his gemstone-like eyes shining brilliantly in the rocking surf.

"Queen Ava," a masculine voice erupts in my head, pulling me from the bliss of transforming with Carter in what felt like our own private world. "You returned."

So much for the merpeople waiting for us on one of the uninhabited nearby islands. Spinning in the water, I peer around and discover only one merman waiting. Tide waves his hand underwater, a gesture taught to him by Giselle one of the few times she met the messenger merman at Celestiana Cove. It took him a while to get used to communicating with his voice and body language, though Giselle didn't mind the surprise welcome kiss right on the lips.

Carter propels us forward to face the merman. All he does is nod at his old friend.

"You're alone," I say.

Tide's brows knit together. "I thought you wanted the others to wait on the island."

I blow a bubble through my lips. "Right, I'm just surprised they listened since they didn't do as Luna asked."

"She's not our queen," he says like it's obvious.

It takes Carter squeezing my hands to stop myself from arguing with Tide about how it shouldn't matter what position Luna is in, because she is the one I seek counsel from and the one I entrust everything to when I'm not available. She's my greatest ally and confidant, and it pains me to see how merpeople treat her because of who her father is. What they don't understand is that Luna was by my side through my worst moments as a mermaid, a time where the colonies still trusted and loved the king. She helped me when no one else could or even would.

I suck in a breath of saltwater. "I know this is an adjustment for everyone, but I'd really—" I pause my thought to Tide. "You know what? It's not important. How about you just lead the way so I can make sure everything is all good?"

Tide offers me a brilliant smile and nods. "It'd be my honor."

With a flick of his tail, he swims forward through the shallows. The reefs teem with too many kinds of fish to count, and Tide surprises me by swimming past a pod of humpback whales. I don't know if it's the excitement of the upcoming full moon or the fact that so many merpeople have taken up temporary residency nearby, but the ocean feels more lively than ever.

"They're here kind of late in the year," Carter says, swimming me close enough to the whales that if I reached my hand out, I could touch one. I don't get the chance, though. Carter jerks me back in time to watch the nearest whale breach from the water, sending us shooting back in the rocky current from its jump.

Bubbles cloud the water, and I wish I could pop up to the surface to get a close up of the show, but a few boat silhouettes pepper the surface.

"Not only the colonies wanting to celebrate," Tide says, sending his thoughts to me. "It's like the sea already knew of your plans to come to Reefaria before the rest of us did."

Something in his words strike warmth in the spark lighting my chest. The ocean works in mysterious ways, and maybe Tide's right. I was gifted with ocean magic to help the merpeople colonies flourish, and with the colonies thriving, so does the rest of the ocean.

"Possibly," I say.

It doesn't take Tide long to guide us to an uninhabited island with turquoise waters, light, almost white sand beaches, and dense greenery hiding who-knows-what on the island's peak. I'm surprised by how few merpeople there are in the bay, but I'm relieved not to be bombarded by hundreds of thoughts all begging for my attention.

I pop to the surface with Carter. Bright sunshine reflects off the rippling water like sparkling starbursts of light. I spit out water and laugh, my voice echoing through the air. It doesn't matter that I've been a mermaid for months, but I'm pretty sure I'll never get over the surprise of how comfortable merpeople are with their bodies.

On the shore in front of me are at least a hundred transformed into human merpeople in various states of dress. It's like we've stumbled upon a nude beach on a deserted island, and I can't stop the blush that splashes my face.

"We'll get the clothing situated," Carter says.

I laugh out of embarrassment because Carter knows me too well. "Never thought I'd experience a naked Christmas."

"Not even with me?" He smirks and slides his arm around my back to pinch the small ridge between my skin and scales.

I dunk my head under to hide my now flaming hot face. Carter's laughter sounds from above me, and a moment later he dips down to smile at me through the swirling bubbles of the moving current.

It takes me a minute to transform into a human and put my bikini bottoms back on. I pop to the surface and spot

Carter's board shorts slung over his shoulder. He's really never going to let me live this down. He's a true merman in moments like these, playfully pointing out how that even though I can turn my legs into a tail, control the sea, and bond forever to one soul, that my human nature is deep seated and will always connect me to the land. The land Carter loves.

I splash him in the face with a magical wave of the sea. "Knock it off."

"Never."

I swim forward without Carter, riding a wave of my making to the shore. I don't even have the chance to rest in the sand before someone picks me up and sets me on my feet. Strong arms wrap around me, and an old, familiar merman kisses my cheeks.

"My Ava! Happy Summer Solstice. I thought I was going to have to wait until the full moon to see you." Pops, Carter's grandfather, squishes me again in another hug.

I giggle, accepting another embrace despite the fact he's wearing only a Speedo. "Of course not. I had to make sure you all weren't causing any trouble."

He laughs. "Says the queen of rule breaking."

Carter comes up behind me, and Pops sandwiches me between him and Carter to give his grandson a hug. A few other merpeople wait in a circle around me, and I go from one pair of arms to another and another with Carter by my side. It's not until I'm finally given some room to breathe that I notice the Christmas tree shaped sand sculpture decorated with sea shells and strands of sea weed. A few merbabes toddle on wobbly legs through the sand watching an older merchild make a sand angel. With how quickly merpeople can pass information to each other through a single kiss, I should've expected they'd adapt some human holiday traditions to their time on land. And I know it's for me.

My eyes blur with tears, and I sniffle.

"Oh, Ava. What's the matter?" Grandmer saunters through the sand from her spot under a hibiscus tree blooming with vibrant red flowers. She closes the distance between us and sticks a flower behind my ear.

I touch the delicate petals. "I'm just so happy. This is better than I could've ever hoped."

A dozen merpeople smile at me. They're much quieter on land than in the sea, some not using their voices at all.

"I hope you don't mind that I showed some people things I know from the land," she says, smiling.

"Of course not. It's perfect. I'm starting to look forward to everything. And when my family arrives—"

"You'll bring them here, too, right?" Grandmer asks, cutting me off.

"They'd love to come." My friends are crazy enough to go with the flow of a bunch of naked merpeople on a deserted island, but I can just imagine the looks on my parents' and their friends' faces. Could be hilarious, though.

"We'll make a trip to the store," Carter says, reading my mind.

I shrug. "I've managed with the adjustment."

He grins, shaking his head. "I love you, Aves."

His words bring a smile to my face, and I take in the small island for a few more minutes. Some of the merpeople eat the hibiscus flowers from the trees while others make temporary camps along the shore. The setup is similar to Celestiana Cove, and it's nice to see how quickly merpeople adjust. Except one thing is missing.

The ocean's protection.

The hum of a boat engine sounds through the quiet air, sending fear into my heart. If someone were to spot us, I'd have a lot of explaining to do since the others would expect me to take charge. Now I feel like a failure once again for not planning ahead. It'd be different if it were just a few of us. We could easily disappear. But there are over a hundred transformed merpeople on the shore and not enough time to reenter the water where we'd be safe.

I do the only thing I can think of. Inhaling a deep breath of sea air into my lungs, I summon the strength of the sea into my fingers. Carter touches my shoulder and points at the small boat in the distance. It's not heading in our direction, but I need to create a magical barrier just in case. It's too close for comfort.

Tropical water rushes my feet as I head back into the docile waves. I touch my fingers to the surface, creating a current to encircle the island with the magic the ocean bestowed on me, willing only those loyal to merpeople to get within reach of us.

I release a small breath and turn to Carter. "Remind me

that I need to always protect everyone first before I get carried away with everything else. The ocean might protect us but the land doesn't."

He stiffens next to me. "But it will try. Look."

I follow Carter's line of sight, my heartbeat pounding in my ears, and a chill icing my bones despite the balmy air. I can no longer hear the sound of the boat, but it's not because it disappeared. Smoke billows from the surface of the water as the boat capsizes a few miles from shore.

"Oh, no," I whisper. "I have to help them."

"And then what?" Carter asks.

If only I knew. The only thing I do know is that this is all my fault. And I have to fix it no matter the costs.

10

STUCK

"FASTER, CARTER," I THINK, CLUTCHING onto my mate's shoulders.

"If someone sees the smoke, there won't be anything we can do," he says back, jetting through the water.

I hate to admit that Carter's right. The smoke will draw attention, and we can't have a rescue team combing the water for the missing people if we have to take them. Our sparks protect us, but I still can't be too careful. The merpeople are too excited, too antsy, maybe even a little careless. They definitely enjoy the newfound freedom that came with my leadership.

I flick my hand out, creating a current to clear the ocean life crowding the water before us. It takes just minutes to reach the boat, but Carter stops short. Three pairs of legs tread water a few feet from the sinking vessel, and I let go of Carter.

"Ava, you shouldn't surface as a mermaid," Carter says, grabbing my wrist.

"I don't have a choice. I have to help them."

I yank from Carter and swim up to reach air. Before I can break through, a series of cramps rush from my back and into my tail, and panic laces around my heart. I did not will myself to transform. I shouldn't be transforming into a human. Nothing has even set me off.

"Carter," I think to him, but it's too late. He can't hear me.

My lungs burn with every passing second, and one of the humans dips underwater, unable to stay afloat. I realize then that the man doesn't have a life vest on. Carter grabs my shoulders, shaking me so that I look into his eyes. He waves his hands at my bare legs, gesturing for me to transform back into a mermaid.

Closing my eyes, I try to force the change to take hold, but nothing happens. It's like the ocean is forcing me to remain human. And I can't stay under for much longer. I point to the surface and push away from Carter. His eyes widen, and his blurry form bends forward as he clutches his tail. Then he transforms into a human, too.

Something triggered both our changes, and it has nothing

to do with a lack of control or our emotions. This is the ocean forcing us to the surface.

I kick my legs, now holding Carter's hand, and we head to the suddenly dark surface together. Smoke clouds the air, and I cough and spit out water only to gag and choke on the putrid smell. My lungs scream with hard to come by breaths, and it's nearly impossible to breathe.

With a wave of my hand, I summon a wave and push it toward the burning boat. Sea water cascades over the vessel, extinguishing the flames, and sending the boat to the ocean floor not far below us.

Something pulls on my leg, and I startle, nearly jumping out of my skin. I peer down and expect to see someone from the colonies, but it's the human man struggling to swim back to the surface.

"Carter, he's drowning." My voice sounds over the hum of the sea, and Carter dives under and pulls the man back to the surface, kicking his powerful legs to keep them both afloat.

A small cry sounds through the air, and I turn my attention to a girl a few years younger than me. She splashes next to an unconscious woman, doing her best to keep the woman's head above water.

"Are you hurt?" I ask, swimming through the rocky water toward the girl.

She only responds by shaking her head.

"Can you swim?" I ask next. The air clears of the lingering smoke as it catches on a sea breeze and dissipates.

She nods.

"Okay, great. There's an island not far from here. Just stay by my side. Everything's going to be okay." I spin in a circle until I spot Carter behind me. "We have to take them."

He puckers his lips, clearly torn between the rules he's known all his life under the reign of Attilonious and the rules I seem to create on a whim. "Whatever you feel is right."

"Let's transf—" Before the words escape my lips, a wave rushes over my head, cutting me off. I knew the ocean would protect us from humans, but it's making it incredibly difficult to fix my own mistake. I pop back to the surface and cough. "Can you manage to swim...like this?"

Carter kicks his legs, pulling the groggy man forward. "The girl can hold onto me, too."

The girl doggy paddles closer and hooks her arms around Carter's neck. I swim the best I can, pulling the woman with me, keeping her head above water. I use a current made of ocean magic to help us swim the distance to the cove of the small deserted island.

Tide pops up from the water next to me in the shallows. "Queen Ava, let me help you." I realize he's utterly human from the smoothness of his arms, lacking his usual pectoral fins.

I hand the woman over to him, and then Pops splashes to the surface to help Carter with the man and girl. The eerie quiet of the shore digs into me, and I jerk my head up to look around, thinking that the rest of the colonies abandoned the land for the sea. But nothing has changed. Everyone stands on shore in their human forms in utter silence, just watching everything unfold. There aren't any merpeople in the water at all.

"I need a healer," I say, kicking through the waves. "The woman hit her head."

No one responds.

"Please, get a healer," I say again.

"Ava," Carter whispers. "I don't think a healer is going to be able to help."

I jerk my head toward him. "What? Why?"

"Because no one can change. We're stuck as humans."

My eyes widen. "Oh, no. This can't be happening."

"What do you think we should do?" he asks.

I rub my hands over my temples. "I don't know. I just—" I pause and glance at the humans we rescued to the merpeople in various stages of dress stuck in their human forms. "I need to go for a swim."

"We're going too far. What are you planning to do, swim all the way to the beach house?" Carter asks, keeping my pace though I know he can swim so much faster.

"If I have to, yeah. But I'm going to pray that the ocean doesn't want to see us drown, so we'll be able to transform if we're far enough away." I swim a few more feet and then stop to tread water next to him. "And if it doesn't, maybe someone will rescue us."

"Or you could train a whale or something to take us the rest of the way," Carter says, smiling.

I splash water in his face. "You think this is a joke? Everyone on that island can't transform into merpeople, and they're freaking out."

His smile melts into a frown, and he reaches out and laces his fingers through mine underwater. "I know it's not a joke. You're just—I love you when you're like this."

"Freaked out?"

"Determined."

I pout my bottom lip, trying not to smile. "Save the gushiness for later when I really need it for ruining the solstice."

"You didn't ruin anything."

"Tell that to the merpeople when they overthrow me."

He chuckles. "Good thing we have our human lives to fall back on."

"Carter..."

He closes the distance and kisses me. "Come on, Aves. We'll get things worked out."

"Maybe with a Christmas miracle."

He laughs again, kissing me once more. Ocean water splashes between us, and I finally pull away to start swimming again. Carter swims ahead of me, leading the way, since any sense of direction is lost to me. The prettiest shade of turquoise water surrounds us for as far as I can see. The sea teems with life below, but my heart hangs heavy in my chest, because my merpeople aren't among the silhouettes crowding the water.

We swim for another mile before I have to stop to rest again. I sink under, letting the tropical water wash over my head, blocking out the hum of the current and the wind. I've never wanted to be a mermaid so badly until this moment. The despair coursing through my very essence must be how it feels to renounce my spark and everything the ocean has given me. Or to feel like Attilonious and have everything ripped away.

Cramps seize my legs, crawling from my feet to my spine, and I release the air from my lungs, watching the bubbles travel to the surface. My cerulean scales glitter on my tail like diamonds are encrusted in the surface. My hair veils the water in front of me, and I spin around once, drinking the sea into my lungs.

I was right about the distance and the ocean. Whatever magic I used is limited to the deserted island.

I pop to the surface and spit out saltwater over Carter's head. He doesn't wait for me to say anything before he sinks under and transforms into the form he feels the most powerful in. Hands wrap around the base of my tail, just above my expansive caudal fin, and Carter pulls me under the water.

His jeweled eyes sparkle like the sea around us. "What now?" he thinks to me.

"We need to figure out what to do about the people we rescued. The ocean obviously didn't want us to reveal ourselves for some reason," I say.

"Celestiana Cove?" he asks.

I shake my head. "I swore to never leave people there. I won't do it."

"Ava, we might have to."

"No. Never again. I'll figure it out."

I just hope I can soon. Because the full moon is coming, and I'm afraid what the ocean will do to those poor people when every mermaid is called back to the sea.

11

A FAMILY AFFAIR

MY KNEES HIT THE BEACH outside our vacation house, and I plop on my stomach and press my cheek into the soft sand. Carter kneels next to me, rubbing his hand across my lower back. The sun set a few hours ago, and the almost full moon shines overhead, taunting me.

"Ava? Carter? I was about to come looking for you." Luna stands on the pathway up to the beach house, a waterproof bag slung over her shoulder. Streaks of silver shine in her black hair from the moon, and her sapphire eyes glitter like the night ocean.

I blow out a breath, sending sand away from my mouth. "Can you transform?" I ask without saying anything else. Carter and I don't need the sea stone rings to transform, but Luna does.

She shifts on her feet. "Uh, why? I haven't done so today, so I don't know."

I release another breath and push off the ground to sit next to Carter. "Can you go try?"

She hesitates. "Sure, I guess."

Without any more questions, Luna saunters into the surf and swims out until she can submerge her head underwater. Her golden tail cuts through the waves as she dives. I scramble to my feet and jump up and down, elation coursing through me. I feared that I ruined this whole mermaid life thing for the whole ocean, but it looks like it's been contained to the island.

But how do I fix it?

"So, now will you tell me what's going on, Ava?" Luna plops down next to me. I was so focused on my own thoughts that I had no idea she had already transformed back into a human.

I stare at the foaming night waves. "Have I ever told you leading the merpeople is hard? Like, I want to quit after the holidays. Think the ocean will accept my resignation?"

Luna touches my knee. "As long as I'm not your replacement, because I'm pretty sure I'd be the most hated queen of the sea."

I shift to look at her. "I have you beat. I'm about to be the most hated on the shore, too. Because as of right now, we have the majority of the colonies stuck in their human forms on a deserted island we can't get close to as mermaids."

She blinks, trying to process my words. "What?"

I lift and drop my shoulders. "Yeah, I kind of saved some humans, and it looks like they're not on the list of people who get to share our secret. My magic basically forced everyone into human forms and won't let them back in the water."

"Oh, my Ocean," Luna says, digging her feet in the sand. "Are you sure?"

"Definitely. And I have no idea what to do."

"Ava! You're here!" a familiar voice rings out.

"Ava-babe! Carter! You guys just wash ashore? Where have you been? I wanted one of you to take me out earlier for a swim. We were warned about jellyfish, and now Sapphire won't even go near the water." Matty jogs onto the beach kicking up sand. Giselle follows behind him, wearing just her bikini and a pair of cotton shorts. "You better tell her that you've told all your fish friends to leave us alone."

I groan.

"Fish friends?" Luna asks. "Jellyfish don't exactly have big personalities. And they taste awful."

Matty laughs. "So, you've seen some around here?"

Luna dusts sand off her legs, tilting her head up to look at Matty. "Actually, no. It's the emptiest I've seen the ocean in a while."

"Is it because the solstice?" Giselle asks, speaking up. "I wanted to snorkel, but if there's nothing to look at..."

"I sunk a boat, saved some people, and now all the merpeople are humans," I blurt. "And I need a mermaid healer, but no healer can get close enough in their form."

Giselle bends down to hug me. "It's a good thing a human doctor doesn't need kick ass mermaid skills to help someone."

"My dad!" I yell. I've been so caught up with all things mermaid that I forgot that my dad should have definitely been on the top of my list of people who can help me. I don't need ocean magic to help anyone. Just family and friends. "Where is he?"

Before anyone can answer me, I'm up on my feet and running toward the houses. Laughter sounds through the air, from the open windows, and I pause on the front porch. I'm about to mess up the start of my family's vacation.

Taking a deep breath, I compose myself the best I can. It'd be much worse if I ran inside freaking the hell out. It's going to be hard enough explaining everything to my parents, who just wanted a nice beachy Christmas with their two daughters and friends.

A light flicks on and my mom peers at me through the glass door. She opens it for me and stands back. "Avie, I wasn't expecting to see you until the morning. Luna said you and Carter went for a swim." She makes it sound like we were at the pool.

I shift on my feet. "Where's Dad?" Might as well get

straight to the point.

"Ava, my girl!" A booming, masculine voice calls from my right, and I spot Mateo coming from what I guess is the living area. I haven't seen the inside of my parents' beach house. "How's everything? The pods coming together and behaving for you?"

I swallow, my throat now dry at the thought. "I—"

"You're here, Avie. Giselle was worried you wouldn't come to shore tonight. All the kids are next door having fun." This comes from Anaya, Giselle's mom.

I blink a few times and watch saltwater drip from my hair and onto the pristine tile. Ruby and Carlton King, Sapphire's parents come into the foyer next, and everyone starts talking to me at once. Their excitement battles with my panic, and I'm not greeted by the one person I need.

"Ava? Ava, what's the matter." Mom touches my arm, pulling my attention from the others and to her.

"I—" My hands shake.

A warm hand touches my shoulder. "Aves."

I spin and face Carter. He frowns, giving me a once over, probably feeling panic and guilt flooding from me and onto him. The edges of my vision darken, the chaos of everyone's holiday cheer and excitement burrows into me, causing my knees to tremble. It's like my legs don't want to be legs in this moment. My heart pulls me to the sea where I know I can think and push away all the distractions.

"Aves..."

I groan, glancing from Carter and over my shoulder at the others. Mom calls my name, but I ignore her because my legs don't just shake, they tingle, too.

"Oh, Ocean. Ava your arm—" Starla comes up next to me and runs her fingers over my pectoral fin.

The room falls silent as everyone realizes what's happening. Warmth creeps from my spark and into my cheeks because the only people apart from my merpeople family to have seen me mid-change are Giselle, Bailey, and Wes.

Dad's voice cuts through the silence as he emerges from the hall. "What's going—"

Carter scoops me into his arms, interrupting my dad's question, and runs me out the door and toward the beach. My lungs burn with each breath, my body craving—needing—the ocean. Scales travel up my legs, sparkling in the white moonlight overhead.

Carter charges into the water, ripping off my bikini bottoms before my tail does it for me, and I push away from him and dive under. This is the ocean's doing. This is the ocean's fault that I'm suddenly transforming again.

I inhale a breath of sea water, letting it cool the fire burning in my chest. I float among the waves on my stomach, not even traveling deep enough to turn upright. I pop to the surface and spit out water. Voices echo over the waves from the beach, and I force my fear away. It's only my parents, Carter's parents, Luna, Giselle, Bailey, and Wes. Thankfully, everyone else decided to stay inside instead of making my embarrassment worse.

Carter touches my hand, still in his human form. "What happened in there, Aves?"

I wipe ocean spray from my face. "Everyone was just so happy, and I didn't want to ruin the first day of their vacation."

"You're not ruining anything," he says. It's a flat out lie to make me feel better, but I press my lips together to stop myself from calling him out.

"Ava, Carter. Can you two please come to shore and tell us what's going on?" Starla calls, standing partially in the surf away from everyone.

I consider diving back into the shallows. I would if Carter wasn't holding onto me.

"Want me to tell them?" Carter asks.

I shake my head. "No, it should be me. You can't always be the one to deliver the bad news."

He kisses my head. "It's not that bad."

"It's worse."

I transform back into my human form, and Carter nearly drags me from the waves to the shore. I wobble on my feet, my body trying to adjust to the sudden back and forth changing, and Carter steadies me.

"Mom, Dad—I—"

Dad holds his hand up to me, and I realize he's on the phone.

Mom closes the distance and wraps her arms around me despite the fact that I'm soaking wet. "Luna told us everything, and Dad's securing a boat for us now. We'll get everything worked out, okay? We're here for you no matter what."

I stand in surprise, taking in my family, both human and merpeople. Mateo wraps his arms around both me and my mom and squeezes us.

"I don't know about everyone else, but I love a good adventure on my vacations," Mateo says.

"Beats being poolside," Giselle adds.

Bailey exaggerates a sigh "Wouldn't feel like Christmas to me without the deserted island, I guess."

I laugh. "I'm going to make it up to you. I swear."

Dad clears his throat, drawing our attention to him. "Everything's set. We can leave port in an hour, Ava."

I nod. "I'm sorry, Dad. I was just trying—"

"No need to explain, Avie. We're all family. This is what we do."

"You didn't have to come, you know," I say, glancing between Giselle, Bailey, and Wes. I couldn't talk Carter's parents or Luna out of coming with us, either. Even Mom decided to come. It's a real family affair.

"What better people to have with you to help deal than someone with the experience of being trapped by the ocean on a deserted island?" Bailey says. She's right. I just hope the merpeople, along with the humans we saved, won't have to stay on the island much longer. But first, we must treat the humans who are hurt. Second, I have to figure out why the ocean did what it did to protect us. Why sink the boat and force a human transformation on everyone?

"Yeah, plus if all else fails, I know how to throw a great beach party," Giselle says with a laugh.

I roll my eyes. "I guess I'll be the one getting the party supplies."

The seemingly endless turquoise ocean goes on for miles and miles, the faint outline of an island in the far off distance. I stand at the bow of the boat, training my eyes on the clear water, half expecting it to rise up to face me. But I'm not so lucky. The last time I even had a semblance of communication with the ocean was through the life essence of the former queen, Luna's mother, Celestiana. But she lives in my memories now, the ocean freeing her magic to live completely within me.

"We can always count on you, Aves," Giselle says with another laugh. Her never ending positive attitude helps ease some of the anxiety gripping my chest.

Strong hands slide around my waist, and Carter presses into my back, resting his chin on my shoulder. He hasn't said much since boarding the vessel and has stayed with Mateo most of the time, who navigates the water as the captain of the boat my dad rented.

"Mom thinks we should swim ahead to scope out the sea," Carter whispers. It still kind of weirds me out that he speaks of Starla like she's both our Mom, but I don't mention it.

"Why? Is something the matter?" I've had enough time swimming to last me a while.

He releases a small breath. "No, but she's having a feeling."

"A feeling? Good or bad?"

"Just a feeling. She said she'll swim alone, but I want us to go with her."

I bob my head. "Whatever you think is right."

He kisses my cheek. "I don't even know what is right these days, but I'd rather be prepared if something's changed."

"Hopefully it has. Besides you, change is one of the only few things I can count on."

Carter hugs me again, pressing his muscular chest into me even more. He lifts me from my feet without warning and dives off the side of the boat, taking me with him. Water engulfs us, thousands of tiny bubbles bursting through the sea, clinging to me while I transform. Carter kisses me the second after I inhale a breath of the ocean, and we stare at each other in the shadow of the boat.

Something nudges my tail, and I half expect to see Starla swimming below us, but a dolphin pup circles around us before jetting back to its small pod. They don't bow-ride like the more playful dolphins I've encountered, who love to surf the waves created by boats, but they stay just close enough to me out of curiosity. I smile, pulling away from Carter, and the baby dolphin swims closer again. It stays with me for a few seconds before bolting away.

"I'm surprised he doesn't want to play," I say to Carter. While sometimes dolphins can be overly friendly with me, this pod is acting unusually shy. Maybe they know what I've done with my magic and are afraid.

Carter grabs my hand and tugs me closer, reaching his hand out. The dolphin calf swims closer again and nudges its round head with nearly no beak against Carter's palm. "Snubfin dolphins are incredibly shy, even with merpeople. I'm surprised they've remained this close."

"I guess their curiosity is getting the best of them," I say, extending my hand out to rub my fingers across the dolphin's smooth back. The rest of the pod closes the distance, surrounding us, and I laugh when an older female basically kisses my cheek.

I wish I could breach from the water, grab Giselle from the boat, and give her a giant pocket of air to be able to experience this with me. I wish I didn't have to fix the mess I caused so I could just enjoy the ocean and give my best friend her exclusive Great Barrier Reef tour.

Bubbles erupt in the water as someone jumps from the boat, causing the snubfin dolphins to dive away from us and disappear through the swirling sand in the now rocky current. Starla appears before us, her dark brown hair drifting behind her. Streaks of moonlight reflect off her glittering aqua tail, and she greets me with a frown.

I grimace right back at her—not because of why we're here but because she scared my new friends away. I need little blips of happiness to get through with knowing I have a lot to fix. The colonies will get incredibly antsy as the full moon nears, especially since most aren't used to remaining in human forms the days before.

Starla reaches out and brushes her fingers through my floating hair, pushing it from my face. "We'll get this all sorted out, even if it means Attilonious gets a few new companions."

I shake my head. "No, Starla. I'm not sending people to island jail because of my mistake. They don't know our secret."

"Don't you think the ocean is being clear about things?"

I narrow my eyes. "Actually, yes. It's giving me a chance to fix this so I don't have to resort to what that tyrant forced to happen to my sister."

She presses her lips together. "I hope you're right."

"Mom, don't doubt my mate," Carter says.

Starla releases a small bubble from her mouth, and it floats toward the surface. "I don't. I just want you both to be prepared."

I huff out a breath of ocean and spin around to swim away. Starla and I haven't always seen things the same way, but I'm afraid she might be right, though I pray to the ocean she isn't. I bolt through the water in the direction of the deserted island, swimming around the suddenly crowded sea. Below me, I spot a few white tip reef sharks hunting for their next meal. I consider joining them in the frenzy and giving up my mermaid duties altogether.

"Ava, don't let her get to you," Carter says, swimming up next to me. I couldn't out swim him to be alone if I wanted to.

"I think she might be right, though. What if I turn into Attilonious 2.0?"

He laughs out loud in the water, sending a stream of bubbles to the surface. "Stop being ridiculous. That will never happen."

I glare, about to argue with him, but a sudden current rips me away and toward the surface. Cramps rush through my legs, and I arch my back, tensing as the setting moon lights up the entire surface in silver ripples. My head cuts through the water, and I gasp, rising from the sea. A massive wave hugs me, lifting me higher and higher as the ocean pushes me from its depths. Voices echo through the air and someone screams. I flick my hands out, willing the wave to freeze. Fear winds around me, squeezing my chest with every breath of sea air, and I finally orient myself to realize I'm hovering in a wave headed directly for the fishing boat with my family on it.

The wave shudders around me, struggling against my ocean magic. I can't hold it for much longer. "Get ready!" I yell, pain burning through me. I fight against the power of the wave reminiscent of the overthrown, tyrant king's making.

My magic falters, releasing the wave, and I scream out. The ocean swallows me, and the last thing I see is the almost full moon shining on the water.

12

WORLD AT RISK

THE ANGRY CURRENT SWAYS ME back and forth among the cloudy sea, sand and bubbles swirling through the water. I push my hands through the ocean, trying to break the glittering, magical barrier I accidentally created before the boat collided against it, but my lungs burn from the lack of air, and I can't focus.

I can't even transform.

In my human form, I can barely manage to kick my legs as I'm tossed about. The ocean doesn't bend to my will, because it isn't under my control like it was for the former king. I'm at the sea's mercy, and if it doesn't want me doing something, it makes it quite clear. And in this moment, it doesn't want me messing with the magic it had bestowed on me.

Arms wrap around my torso, yanking me from the barrier I'm sure surrounds the island. It's not unlike the protective magical fields I've seen both Attilonious and Celestiana create to keep people in and out of places. I hate I'm the one responsible, but I hate more that the ocean's power has turned on me and my family. It could very well sink the boat and swallow us all into its depths.

My head cuts through to the surface, and I gasp deep breaths. The rough waves rock me back and forth, and then the sea suddenly lowers and the water stills like it wasn't trying to drown me moments ago.

"Carter? Oh, God," I say, my voice echoing through the air.

Water splashes over my shoulder. "I'm right here."

"My family," I say.

"We're okay, Aves!" Giselle's voice rings through the air, sending a cold waterfall of relief over my hot panic.

I spin to look behind me, kicking my legs even though Carter's treading is enough to keep the both of us afloat. About fifty feet away, the boat bobs on the water, still adjusting to the sudden calm of the sea. Luna and Giselle float nearby, and I spot Bailey and Wes still clinging to the bow's railing. Mom, Dad, and Mateo rush onto the deck and peer around.

"Ava, girl. We can't sail any further," Mateo says.

Starla pops up not far from Giselle. "We can't swim in our true forms either. How far until the island, Carter?" I realize both Starla and Luna are mermaids while Carter and I are in our human forms, a glittering line of magic separating us.

"I had to swim the surface at Ava's pace and lost track. Her magic far exceeds what Attilonious had possessed, so I'm guessing the barrier extends a few miles," Carter says. A few miles? It felt like a million.

"Miles? Oh, dear. I don't think I can swim that far," Mom says.

I hold onto Carter's shoulders, so I can stop kicking. "I want everyone except my dad to stay here with Mateo and the boat."

"Hey, I'm already in the water," Giselle says, arguing with me.

I flick my gaze to Carter, who twists his lips to the side. The last thing I need is to put more people in danger. What if what happened with the boat and the protective barrier happens in the open water? What if we're separated?

"Don't even think about telling me no. Luna's already agreed to be my swimming buddy," Giselle adds.

I glower at her. "Fine, but you have to wear a life jacket." I turn my attention to my dad. "You too, Dad. Carter will be swimming you there."

Sure, it's kind of awkward to have my dad hold onto my mate's back like some kind of trained ocean animal, but Carter's the person I trust most with my dad's life.

"And you'll be with me, Ava," Starla says, speaking up. "Your dad might need some assistance."

As much as I want to argue, I don't. Starla would ignore me if I told her to stay with Mateo anyway. She's a gifted mermaid healer, and even if she needs to be a mermaid to really use her talent, she can still help as a human. Plus, she does know a thing or two. I won't tell her that, though.

"Okay, so everything's set," I say. "Dad, hand your bag to Carter and jump in when you're ready."

Carter leaves me to swim to the stern of the boat to wait for my dad. Dad pulls off his shirt, folds it, and stuffs it into his bag, and then straps on his lifejacket. He drops the bag to Carter but doesn't jump in right away.

He stares at the water for a long moment. "I think I see a shark, Avie." My dad was never much of an ocean enthusiast or very adventurous for as long as I can remember, so I don't blame his hesitation.

Carter sinks under and peers around. He pops back up with a splash. "Just some resting reef sharks. Nothing to worry about."

My dad still hesitates.

I swim closer. "Come on, Dad. We're fine. The sharks don't ever bother us. Mermaids don't have predators in the ocean, even in human form. Even then, the chances of getting bit are low. Trust me, okay?"

He inhales a deep breath of the sea breeze, his chest puffing out. Closing his eyes, he jumps from the stern of the boat and into the water. Carter helps him to the surface and treads in place next to him.

"Water's warm," Dad says, wiping it from his face.

I laugh. I can't help it. "All good?"

He nods. "Lead the way."

"Queen Ava! You've returned." Warm hands yank me from the sand and pull me to my feet. Sun, Reefaria's top advisor, steadies me, holding onto my arm to make sure I don't fall flat on my face.

I teeter in place, exhaustion settling in my very bones. "I had no idea you had left Reefaria, Sun. I was hoping you hadn't."

"Of course I came. I just—I couldn't stay in the colony. The pull was too strong." He steps away from me and kicks up a leg, his golden hair shining. "And look at this! I'm moving about so much better than last time. I had no idea you wanted us all on land before solstice. What a marvelous idea."

I place my hands on my hips, keeping my gaze on Sun's wide eyes. "Well, it wasn't exactly the plan. I was only trying to protect you from the humans. Where are they anyway?"

"The Swanson pod? Lovely humans. Don't talk much." Sun's voice grows louder with every word. "Which is so strange. It's so—amazing? Yes, amazing—to hear this noise coming from me."

"Can you show me where they are?" Dad steps up next to

me, his bag dangling from the crook of his arm. The others stand silently nearby.

"You brought Dr. Adair. And Giselle!" He leaves me to face my best friend. "Oh, Giselle, how lovely you are this morning. Your hair shines with all the warmth of the sun."

Giselle full on giggles. "Why, thanks."

"The humans?" Dad asks again. He steps closer to Sun so that the merman has to focus on him.

"Oh, right. This way." Sun motions for us to follow him.

Giselle doesn't move from her spot. The second we make eye contact, her eyes gloss over before they crinkle in the corners and she bares her teeth in a silent squeal. Seeing her reaction to the merman's attention makes me laugh, and my voice sounds through the air.

Starla narrows her eyes at me, and I slap my hand over my mouth. Giselle laughs next, and if I didn't have to follow behind my dad, I'd stay with her in the sand to gossip about how Sun just gave her a compliment like he would give a potential mate.

Carter links his fingers through mine, tugging me along. I watch Luna hug Giselle, and Giselle shake her head. Without having to ask, I know Giselle has no interest in becoming the mate of Reefaria's most prestigious elder. I don't blame her. Reefaria is a long ways from La Tortuga Point and Azure Waters.

"That was interesting," Carter says, knowing exactly what I'm thinking about.

"Funny, too. Gi would never consider—"

"You sure about that?"

"Isn't he in his thirties?"

"When you live as long as us in the water, age isn't a big deal. Mermen are patient," he says.

I snort. "I don't think so, Carter."

He nudges my shoulder, jerking his chin to look behind us. I catch sight of Giselle looking in our direction, but not at us—at Sun. Oh, boy.

"You know the stories about sirens luring sailors to sea?" he asks, smiling. "Mermen can be persuasive, too. And we're known for romance. There could very well be a transformation and coupling ceremony for you to plan in the near future."

I flick his arm and laugh. "Stop making me laugh. It's hard to focus on the disaster I've created."

"No way. I'm your mate. It's my job to stop you from worrying so much."

"Carter..."

"Just think of the merbabes Giselle and Sun could have."

"Carter!"

He chuckles, covering his mouth with his hand to muffle the sound. Sun and Dad stop in front of us, and I pull away from Carter to come up next to them. The scent of smoke wafts through the air, and I peer down at the three humans we pulled from the water sitting around a camp fire and eating some sort of cooked fish from on top of heart-shaped, hibiscus tree leaves.

"Our queen has arrived," Sun says, his words drawing the

family's attention to me. "And she brought a healer."

I cringe, clenching my jaw at the fact that Sun just introduced me as a queen.

The man gives me a once over. "Queen? What is going on?"

Dad steps in front of me and extends his hand. "I'm Dr. Adair, and this is my daughter Ava. I heard your boat capsized offshore. I'd like to give you a physical exam before we discuss anything further." I don't know if it's because he's my dad or because of the man's tone, but he's taking control of the situation just like he would back home. It's something I appreciate. I might be the merpeople's queen, but I kind of just want and need my dad to take charge.

The man purses his lips. "I—"

"Mum's hurt, Dad." It's the first time I've heard the girl speak. She was so in shock when we found her that she didn't say a word.

"She'll be right, Caitlin." The man's Australian accent thickens the louder and more wound up he gets. "I'll borrow your boat if ya have one, mate."

"Dad," the girl, Caitlin, says again.

"My head hurts, Samuel. Let the doctor take a look," the woman says.

"You can see a real doctor when we get off this island, Sarah," Samuel says, waving around the shore. "The mozzies are eating me alive." He smacks an imaginary mosquito on his leg.

I take a deep breath, because I'm sure I'm about to piss him off at any second with what I'm about to say next. "You can't leave. Not now. I'm sorry."

"What?" the man asks.

Carter steps in front of me protectively. "Ava means that we don't have a boat at the moment."

"Not even a tinny? How'd ya get here?"

"They swam," Caitlin says, answering for me. "I saw them come ashore. It's how they rescued us, too."

Samuel snaps his head up to really look at us—and I mean *really* look at us. You'd think I was lounging on the beach with my glittering tail with the way he studies my sandy legs. I shift on my feet, digging my toes into the powdery sand.

He jerks his attention to my dad and points his finger at him, his eyes widening. "You have a lifejacket on!"

Dad messes with the strap. "Because I can't swim as well as the others on this island."

"And who are the others here? You sound American."

"We're on vacation," Dad says. "Ava said you might need a doctor so she brought me here."

"From where?"

"A b—"

I raise my hand and cut off Dad before he can tell Samuel that we do have a boat offshore. "It doesn't matter. As soon as you allow my dad to do his job, we'll figure things out. Your wife is bleeding." I hadn't seen the blood until the woman leaned forward and laid her face to her knees. "I think she needs stitches."

Before I realize what's happening, Samuel jumps to his feet and launches at my dad. Carter tugs him back, spinning him around to shield him from Samuel. Sun reaches out and grabs the man by his wrinkled T-shirt, and something in me snaps. With a flick of my hand, I pull a small wave from the surf and send a waterfall of saltwater over Samuel's head, surprising him.

"What was that?" he asks, yelling so loudly that birds take flight from the nearby trees.

I straighten my shoulders. "It was a wave."

"The beach is fifty feet away."

I shrug.

His forehead wrinkles, a glower crossing his face. Sun holds him in place. I inhale a deep breath to stop from pulling another wave from the ocean to drop on him, because with the way he looks at me, you'd think I'm some sort of wicked witch—or evil siren.

"Tell me what's going on before I—"

"Sun, please take Samuel for a walk until he calms down," I say. "My dad can't help his mate if he's all worked up."

"What! No!" Samuel screams. "You can't make me go."

I turn my attention to Samuel's wife and daughter, clearly frightened by the whole situation. I don't blame any of them for their emotions. I'm not sure how I'd feel to have had my boat sink in open water, be rescued by swimmers, and then left on an island with no escape with hundreds of people in various stages of dress who don't exactly follow any human social norms.

"Sarah, love! Do something. They'll kill me," Samuel

screams.

I kneel by Caitlin and touch her hand. "No harm will come to your dad. We're just trying to help out, and I'm afraid his fear is going to get someone hurt." I shift to face Sarah. "Mind if my dad looks at the wound on your head? I swear he's an excellent doctor in the states. He's an emergency room surgeon."

The woman glances from me to my dad and nods once. "Yes, ta."

"You're welcome," I say. I hold out my hand to Caitlin. "How about you come with me? I saw some fruit trees not far from here. You're probably hungry since you didn't touch your fish."

Caitlin looks to her mom to see what she should do, and Sarah nods with a nervous smile. The girl takes my hand, and I motion for Carter to stay with Sarah and my dad. We stroll a few feet away, and all the merpeople keep their distances for once, giving us space. If I'm going to help this family, I need to know who and what I'm dealing with, and Caitlin seems like the best and easiest person to give me the answers I need.

"So, you're a queen?" Caitlin asks, watching me in her peripheral vision.

"No, not really. Just a college student. My family came here for Christmas vacation," I say.

"And Summer Solstice. I heard your pod talking. It's much bigger than I thought one would be. I also heard them mention you usually live in a colony," she says.

I freeze. "Um, what?"

"They're excited."

I knew the others wouldn't be able to keep a secret this close to a major holiday when they don't think humans can be a threat. Attilonious always took care of it. Only those who loved the land ever really worried.

"I'm not sure what you're talking about," I say. "But, I would love to know more about your dad."

Caitlin shifts our stroll away from the tree line and to the water. "He likes to fish."

Great. Awesome. Not all fisherman are a threat to us, but there are a whole lot of them who are, the ones who don't re-spect everything in the ocean. Samuel is the reason why the ocean fought so hard to protect everyone, even forcing us into human forms. He really does put my whole world at risk.

"But you don't have to worry about him," Caitlin contin-ues. "He'd never hurt you."

I frown. "He tried to attack my father, who really is a doc-tor by the way."

"So, he's not a merman? Or can mermen live on land?" she asks.

I freeze. "I—" It's not hard to put two and two together, especially if you're open-minded. My parents believed me even before seeing me.

Caitlin reaches down and slaps a rolling wave, splashing me in the face with water. Shock stuns me silent, and all I can think about is running into the sea, but it's not like the ocean would hide me.

I blink and wipe saltwater from my face. "What the hell was that for?"

She takes a step back and raises her hands in surrender. "I'm sorry! I thought you'd change."

"Into a mermaid?" My voice rises through the air. "That's a little out there, don't you think?"

Her lip quivers. "Don't lie to me. I know you're a mermaid. I've seen one of you before, but my mates laughed at me when I told them. But they won't laugh now."

Fear trickles up my spine. "You're mistaken."

"Stop! I'm not. I know what I saw, and you're a mermaid, Ava. Ava—Adair."

My mouth drops open at the use of my full name with her accusation. This isn't good. This is a full on disaster. It wasn't Samuel I should've been worried about. It wasn't Samuel that the ocean was protecting us from.

It was Caitlin, a tween girl with an open mind and a point to prove.

I swallow the burning feeling in my throat, threatening to steal my words away. "Caitlin," I whisper. "Please, you have to listen to me."

"Why, mermaid? Queen Mermaid."

I reach out and press my hand over her mouth. "Shut up!" I hiss. "Do you know what happens to people who try to put our lives at risk?"

"You don't look like a murderer," she says, her voice muffled against my hand.

A shadow falls over us, the sun suddenly darkening out of nowhere. Caitlin screams, pushing me hard, and I fall into the sand.

I yell, waving my hand out, but it's too late.

A massive wave comes crashing down on us, washing Caitlin away from me. It was never me she should've worried about. It was the sea.

And Caitlin's about to drown.

13

WHAT THE SEA WANTS

"CAITLIN!" I SCREAM, RUNNING INTO the surf. Waves pulverize me, washing me back into the trees. My back hits a rough palm, and pain slices through me as my skin rubs against the bark. I hook my arm around the palm tree, keeping myself from getting swept into the sea. Holding my hand up, I concentrate on calming the ocean—not controlling it, but willing it with my very essence to relax.

"Please," I whisper. "Let me fix this."

Like the unforgiving sea hears my prayers, the suddenly

high tide retreats. A figure lies face down in the sand, and I rush over to Caitlin. Voices sound out, and a crowd of merpeople jogs toward us. Carter pushes through, kneeling down next to me, and flips Caitlin onto her back.

He leans down to listen. "She's not breathing."

"Caitlin? Oh, God. Caitlin!" Sarah's voice rips through the air as she screams upon seeing her daughter in the sand.

I hold my hand up, and Tide grabs hold of the woman to keep her from getting in the way. My dad jogs forward, but before he can get within a few feet of us, the ocean swells in a wave and knocks him into the crowd.

I hold my hand above Caitlin and try to pull the sea from her lungs, but nothing happens.

"Queen Ava, the sea wants her," a mermaid with flowing golden hair says. I've only met her a few times, but I know her name is Pearl.

I shake my head. "She's not a threat." I'm not talking to the mermaid. Getting to my feet, I face the endless turquoise water that turns into the same cerulean blue as my tail in the horizon. "Please, don't do this. I know that she poses a risk for us. I know you're trying to protect us. But please, I'm begging you. If you don't let me help her, I'll do exactly what Attilonious wanted and return to sea. We'll never be united."

"Ava," Carter says.

I swipe a tear from my eye. "This is not what I agreed to. I can't just let her die. People can change. She's just a girl."

Silence falls over the island like someone hit the mute button. Even the waves don't hum. Slowly turning around, I face everyone from the colonies. All the merpeople have come to my side to surround me with the love and affection they freely give to me. Each of the sparks in their chests flickers in quick succession, and for the first time ever, they all blink in sync with my own mermaid essence.

"I stand with Ava," Carter says.

"I stand with my queen, too," Luna says.

Voices hum out, cutting through the silence, and all the merpeople start strolling back to the sea in their human forms. Carter puts his hands on my shoulders, standing behind me, and I hover over Caitlin still in the sand. Sun releases Samuel, who hugs Sarah against him, and Dad watches me with glassy eyes. He knows what it means if I follow through with my word.

Giving up the land means giving up my human life completely.

It might very well end here.

"Ava," Giselle says, rushing from Dad's side despite the fact that the ocean can wash her away if it chooses to do so. She splashes in the sea and hugs me. "I don't want to lose you."

I sniffle. "Please, understand. I know our secret is important, and I know I have responsibilities, but I will not pay this sort of price. I'm not Attilonious. My life isn't worth more than anyone else's. I don't care if the ocean gave me magic or a second chance to live my life how I wanted. I just—I can't—not like this."

Giselle rubs her hand under her eyes, takes a deep breath, and then turns to the sea. She jumps in and kicks her legs like she can somehow beat the ocean into submission. "I've always loved you!" she screams. "I've done everything in my ability to do my part in taking care of you and respecting you and all your creatures. You can't do this. You can't take my best friend!"

"My mom gave her life to save you," Luna says, talking to the sea. "She gave up everything! You can't do this to Ava!"

The ocean rises, building a swell taller than the palms. The beach is nearly empty of everyone, the merpeople now in the water, in this massive wave that's trying to intimidate me, to show me how powerful it really is. But I've never denied its power. I've never denied its request.

But now, I have to.

I have to do what's right for me.

Warm fingers lace through mine, and I smile at Carter. Glancing over my shoulder, I meet Dad's wide eyes as he stands frozen in place. Both Luna and Giselle face the towering wave with me and Carter, and it's only a matter of time before it sweeps us all away.

I take a deep breath of the ocean air and step forward.

"Ava, you're a great queen," Starla says. I turn my head to catch sight of Starla standing with Grandmer and Mateo's parents. "A kind and generous queen."

I nod, blinking tears from my eyes. Lifting my hand, I touch my fingers to the wave, feeling the tropical water coat my hand. It sparkles against my skin, now shining with a pearlescent glow. Cerulean scales sprout on my legs, glittering in the pale sunlight beaming through the sea. My sea stone ring catches the light and swirls with the magic the ocean has given to me.

"I'm sorry, Carter. I know how much you love the land," I whisper.

"Not as much as I love you, Aves," he says.

"Forever and ever. No matter the sea or land," I say.

"Always."

Dozens of sparks blink before me in the water. The merpeople of the colonies hover in the rising, crystal wave in their true forms. With one more look to Giselle and my dad, I step forward into the wave with Carter. Sucking a breath of the ocean, I complete my transformation and prepare to swim to my family before the wave washes them away.

But something happens. Magic bubbles in the ocean, sending fragments of light bouncing off the white sand below me and each tiny bubble surrounding me. The wave recedes without crashing forward, and my head cuts through the surface to air. Sun warms my skin, my scales glinting like diamonds.

Caitlin's figure remains in the sand, and I glance from her to the ocean. "Thank you," I whisper.

Placing my hand on her chest, I will for the water to rise from her lungs and back into the sea. The ocean can take a life in seconds, but it also gives and creates life. It stole my life and revived me. It gave me a second chance, just like I'm trying to do for Caitlin.

"Come on," I say to the girl. "Breathe."

Caitlin coughs, and I turn her on her side. She spits and sputters into the sand before taking a deep breath of air. Dad rushes to her side along with her parents, and I just sit back and watch them from my place in the sand.

Caitlin sits up, her eyes widening when she sees me. I expect her to scream, to lash out at me for what the sea had done, but all she does is scramble through the sand on her hands and knees. Carter cuts her off in his merman form, his muscles sparkling with sea spray.

She stops in place. "I knew it! You are mermaids."

"Well, I'm a merman," Carter says, smirking.

I bump his shoulder. "Right. And you know a secret very few people know."

"Whoa," she whispers. "I just—can I be a mermaid? How does that work?"

I furrow my brows. "You have to either be born or chosen. And if you're chosen, you have to drown to become a mermaid. It's actually really unpleasant."

"It also doesn't always work," Carter says.

Her smile falters. "Oh."

"Did I mention that the ocean will kill you if you say anything? Pretty sure it'll sink the entire continent."

Her eyes widen. "What?"

"Yeah, there's an island I can take you to if you insist on proving my existence, too," I add.

"It's actually pretty nice," Giselle says, interrupting. "I lived there over the summer. Ate fish every day. Slept in the sand, sometimes in a cave if it was storming."

"An island? Like this?"

"Except in the Pacific."

"Alone?"

I glance at Caitlin's parents, who are so overloaded with what's happening, they just stand stunned next to my dad. "I can try to keep you together. The ocean didn't deem your parents as a threat."

"I'm not a threat!" Caitlin yells. "You saved me. I owe you my life. Please, I don't want to live on an island. I don't like eating fish."

"Don't tell it to me. It's the sea who's worried," I say.

Caitlin scrambles from the sand and into the surf. A small wave rushes around her, and she stares into the water. I can't hear what she says, but whatever it is, the ocean responds by swirling around her instead of pushing her back to shore.

Turning her head, she looks over her shoulder at me. "Did it work? What did the ocean say?"

I look at Carter, and he shrugs.

"Your call, Aves," he says.

"I think it's all going to be okay," I say. "But you have to promise me that you'll never speak another word to anyone."

"I promise," Caitlin says.

"Okay, great. Let's see about getting you all home. I hope you don't mind swimming for a bit," I say.

"Swimming? How far?"

Giselle taps Caitlin on the shoulder. "Does it matter? You

get to swim with mermaids."

Caitlin laughs and turns to her parents. "This is the best early Christmas present ever."

Carter hugs me from behind and rests his chin on my shoulder. He whispers, "I have something better for you, my queen."

"You do, do you?" I ask.

He grins. "Just wait for tonight."

"Tonight?"

He spins me around and peers into my eyes. "I promise it'll be worth it."

"I bet." I kiss Carter sweetly, letting Dad and Starla take over the situation I've barely managed to escape from.

Hundreds of blinking lights decorate the aqua water, reminding me of everything I've been given this year. Each spark is a gift, a special merperson, a new family member—family I'm willing to give up everything, even the land, for. I think the ocean realized I'll never be like Attilonious, the fallen merman king who'd wipe cities from the map to keep the colonies safe, and that's why it chose me.

Because I love the sea and the land, and I'll do everything I can to unite us for the future I—we—deserve.

14

JUST A LITTLE REMINDER

"OH, OCEAN," I SAY, CUPPING my hands over my mouth. "When did you have time to do this?"

Carter laughs and pulls me from the water and into the dry sand. "I have my ways."

"I love it! It's amazing."

The hum of a generator buzzes through the soft night on the small island not far from the shore of our beach house. Rainbow lights twine around every palm tree for what seems like forever, creating the perfect, beachy Christmas. The most amazing sand sculpture of a snowman sits under the dazzling glow of twinkle lights with a red Santa hat, sunglasses, and a mouth made from sea shells. It's greeting card perfect, and I can't stop the excitement rushing through me.

Carter guides me from the waves, and the buzz of the water disappears as the tinkle of Christmas music sounds through the air. Stockings hang from a bent palm tree, and just past it, a bonfire lights the sand aglow, showing off a couple of expertly wrapped presents.

Then, I see another bonfire and another. If I couldn't see the glitter of ocean magic protecting these shores, I'd run back into the sea before this beacon of light brought every boater to shore.

"What is all this?" I ask.

"A new tradition. A new holiday. With our whole family—land and sea."

I embrace Carter, kissing him softly on the lips. Laughter sounds through the trees, and I notice the shadows of silhouettes moving about.

"Ava!" Luna says, waving to me from under the twinkling lights of a palm tree.

"Surprise!" Giselle says, popping up next to her. "Welcome to the first annual SolMas? ChristSol?"

"Humerpeople Day?" Luna asks.

I crinkle my nose. "I'll let you guys work that out."

They both look at each other and then laugh. Seeing my best friends, one from land and one from sea, together fills me with such love. I'm so lucky to have them in my life. I'm lucky to have everyone in my life.

All I needed was a little ocean magic and my family on my side to get through this solstice and Christmas disaster, which is now a holiday miracle. I could've never imagined a true beachy holiday—a blend of the land and sea—as amazing as this.

Carter plops a Santa hat on my head before adjusting one on his own head, and I laugh when I realized he switched out his blue board shorts for a pair of red ones with a Santa belt dyed into the fabric. It's the cutest, dorkiest thing ever—like a kid on Christmas morning in Santa pajamas full of the Christmas spirit I have to admit I've been lacking.

"Queen Ava, isn't it awesome?" Sun says, kicking up sand as he gets up from next to the fire.

"Awesome?" I ask, smiling.

"Sounds like Gi," Carter whispers.

I elbow him. "It is awesome. Nice board shorts."

He tugs on the side of his checkerboard swim trunks. "A gift from the radiant Giselle."

"Oh," I say, glancing over my shoulder at Giselle. She raises her arms, questioning my expression.

Carter leans into me and whispers, "Sapphire and Matty went shopping with the others while we were gone. Cleared out the swim sections at every store for miles...but Giselle passed them out."

I suck in my bottom lip to stop from laughing. "They're great, Sun."

"She made me this necklace, too. Princess Luna is an excellent teacher," he says.

Oh, boy. "She definitely is."

Carter chuckles, pulling me away from Sun. I peek over my shoulder and watch him join Giselle and Luna, clearly no longer against Luna being my right-hand mermaid, especially since Giselle is her right-hand human.

I soak in the excitement radiating from everyone around, from the merpeople, and my family and friends blended among them. Mom and Dad laugh with Starla and Mateo. Grandmer braids Sapphire's hair while it looks like Matty and Logan are competing against Tide at throwing pebbles in the surf. Daisy and Chloe talk with a few mermaids around a fire.

"This isn't so bad, right?" Bailey comes up next to me, sliding her arm around my shoulders. "I'm proud of you, Avie. Always managing to save the day. Summer Solstice and Christmas day should be a breeze to get through."

"I'm looking forward to the day after when I can just enjoy our vacation. Did you see the list of family activities Ruby posted on our fridge?" I ask.

She laughs. "Apparently we're watching some big mermaid moonlight celebration tomorrow."

I shake my head. "I'll do my best to be entertaining, but then after that, I'm going to find my own deserted island."

"You won't need to," she says, grinning.

I tilt my head to the side. "Why?"

She smiles even bigger. "Because I promised to get Mom

off your back."

I follow her gaze, confusion crinkling my forehead. Wes waves at us, and then climbs onto the bent palm tree to get everyone's attention. The crowd around us falls silent, and Bailey pulls away from me to stand by Wes. Carter slides up next to me, taking her place. He looks as confused as I am. Only Giselle beams a smile bright enough to light the dark beach.

"I'd like to make a toast," Wes says, his deep voice booming through the night. His long hair catches on a sea breeze, flowing behind him. "It was almost nine years ago when I was sitting on the shores of Celestiana Cove, watching the tide roll in when Bailey washed up right at my feet. I didn't know this at the time, but the ocean delivered who I've known for some time to be my mate, my soul mate, and the love of my life. And with Bailey came a miracle I never expected—a chance at a life together outside of an island that imprisoned me. She brought me to all of you, who have been so kind and generous. She has given me a family I thought I'd never have the chance to have. So, I just wanted to make a toast to you all, and a toast to my Bailey, who has agreed to marry me and be my forever mate."

I squeal and rush away from Carter to hug my sister. We rock back and forth, and she holds up her hand to reveal the beautiful, princess-cut diamond glittering on a simple silver band. Mom and Dad steal Bailey away, and she's surrounded and passed around by all the merpeople, chatting excitedly about the queen's sister's coupling ceremony.

Wes jumps from the tree in front of me, and I throw my

arms around him. "Congratulations, Wes. I'm so happy that you'll officially be part of my family. I already considered you my brother, but I just—" I squeal again and squeeze him tighter.

"We'd like to have the ceremony on Celestiana Cove if that's okay. Figured you could officiate, work some ocean magic, you know."

I smile. "I thought you hated that place?"

He shrugs. "It was our home for so long, and we have a lot of good memories there. Plus, it can accommodate all the merpeople."

I laugh. "Really?"

"Yes, really. We wouldn't be here if it weren't for the merpeople," he says. "Plus, they know how to throw a great party."

He's right. I wouldn't be here without the merman who saved me. I glance at my mate, laughing and hugging Bailey. There is nothing better to merpeople than two souls finding each other and coupling.

When Carter catches sight of me, he makes his way over and hugs Wes, welcoming him into our family. Wes heads over to join Bailey, and Carter holds me against him, resting his head on mine.

"You know, seeing Wes and Bailey, feeling their happiness as much as yours—it reminds me how we basically eloped in the sea," he says, shifting.

I turn to meet his dark eyes. "Fancy ceremonies don't matter to me. I'd love you regardless."

He smiles. "Walk with me?"

Carter pulls me away from the crowd, and we meander down the beach to just beyond the last bonfire. Two beach chairs sit in the sand near a glowing, light strung palm tree. Smooth, glittering sea glass sparkles from the sand and shells dangle from the palm fronds like ornaments. A wrapped box rests atop one of the chairs, and I smile at Carter.

"For me?" I ask. "I left your present at the house."

He smiles and pulls the top off, showing off an array of desserts. "For the both of us. From Giselle. But that's not it. I do have something for you."

Carter reaches into his pocket and pulls out a tiny box with a silver bow on top. "I didn't want to take away from your sister's excitement, but I have something for you." He pops open the box and reveals a ring with an emerald cut brown gemstone on it. "This is to make it official on the land—a chocolate diamond."

My mouth forms an O. "Are you asking me to marry you?"

"Well, that's usually what happens on land, right?" he says with a laugh. "I know you wanted to wait until you graduated college, and I'm happy with that, but I'm your mate in the sea and land, and your sea stone deserves something from the land to keep it company."

I smile. "You might be right."

Carter slides the ring on my finger, fitting it perfectly against my sea stone ring, creating the perfect set. "Just a little reminder that the land loves you, too."

I grin and pull him to me, burying my face against his bare chest. "Is this about today when I almost renounced the land to save that girl?"

"Not gonna lie, Aves. I was scared."

I puff out my bottom lip. "Me, too. But it had to be done. She was a child, and I'm not a murderer and I will do everything I can not to abandon some unsuspecting soul on Celestiana Cove."

He kisses my forehead. "Another reason why I love you, my queen, my mermaid mate...my future human wife."

"I like the sound of that," I say.

"Good, because you're stuck with me."

"And I like the sound of that."

15

BEST SOLSTICE EVER

BRIGHT MOONLIGHT CUTS THROUGH THE clear water in silver beams, setting the pearls and shells decorating the rock platform aglow. All the merpeople from all seven colonies throughout the five oceans surround me, their sparks blinking in a beautiful array of light. I take in each face, each tail color, each soft voice humming through my mind in anticipation for the big swim.

The night's been incredible, the joyous emotions palpable. I even managed to survive the feeding frenzy. The solstice feast reminded me of our usual Christmas dinners, where everyone stuffed their faces until they sunk to the couch and then still managed to eat dessert—except replace the couch with the sandy ocean floor and no one having to worry about cleanup since the sharks took care of that.

I straighten my shoulders, fanning out my caudal fin to sweep the platform as I hover in place. Moonlight catches on my silver crown and the pearls and sea glass woven into the sea grass top Luna made especially for me. Carter floats next to me, his arms folded across his chest, and Luna hugs Starla as they watch from the sand in the front row.

With a wave of my hand, I bend the current to scatter sparkling bursts of light across the crowd like tiny stars fallen into the glowing ocean. Merbabes laugh and swim from their parents arms, chasing and playing with the glittering bubbles, and I suck in a deep breath of the sea.

"Tonight is a night I'll always remember. It wasn't long ago that I feared the ocean, the unending depths that left me in constant uncertainty. I feared the idea of losing myself and who I was as a human to the sea. But what I feared the most after the ocean had chosen me was losing my family. In that time, I only thought about what was changing, what was being taken away, and never thinking about what I had been given." I pause and look at Carter.

I offer him a smile. "And I've been given so much. Not only did the ocean not steal my human world, it actually bestowed on me an entire new world to join with the land I cherished. It had extended my family and had given me a gift unlike any other—a chance to help flourish a future for the sea. So tonight, to honor the ocean and every pod in every colony, we will swim the surface, soak in the full moon light, and remember everything the ocean has given us—our homes, our pods, our essences, our mates, and a chance to have a future on land or in the sea."

The crowd cheers, shooting up from the sand to hug and kiss each other. Merbabes circle me in excitement, and I laugh and swing a few around. Starla and Mateo give me a look that speaks volumes about a future they desire for me and Carter, and I force the thoughts away.

Hands slide around my stomach and rest below my naval on the ridge separating my skin from scales. Carter surprises me by swimming me up toward the surface so fast that all I see are the dancing lights. We break through the surface and breach together in the middle of the open ocean with the enormous full moon hanging in the glittering, star-speckled sky above us.

I wave my hand, summoning a wave to catch us. All the merpeople follow suit, and I smile at such a magnificent sight. I sit on the ocean's surface and wave my hands out, freezing the splashes of everyone above the water. Water orbs of all sizes hang in the air, reflecting the moonlight like a glass surface. The orbs glitter through the night like twinkle lights strung on invisible lines, and voices cheer through the air.

I shift to look behind me at the yacht filled with my family and friends. Rainbow lights decorate the railings of the vessel, and I spot Giselle standing next to Caitlin and her family. Carter was hesitant about inviting them to join us on the Summer Solstice, but I thought what better way to guarantee they keep our secret than seeing a bright new world full of magic that they can cherish and respect, a world worth protecting.

"Ready to swim, my queen?" Carter asks, brushing his lips on my neck just below my ear.

I bob my head and smile. "Lead the way, my warrior."

Carter waves at our family on the yacht, and I blow them a kiss. Together, we dive under, the crowd of merpeople parting ways to create a path for us to swim through. Carter's parents and the rest of his family, along with Luna, wait for us at the back on the ground and follow us when we swim through the open ocean.

Carter hooks his arms around me, swimming me faster, and I hold my arms out like we're flying through the sea. He speeds ahead of the colonies, leading the way with me in his arms. I spin, turning my body to face Carter, our sparks blinking in perfect rhythm.

I slide my hands around his neck and kiss him. "Happy Summer Solstice," I say, thinking the thought to him.

He kisses me deeper, sending a wave of love and joy and everything good in the world from him to me. "The happiest. The best solstice ever."

"Are you sure you don't want an exclusive tour of the Great Barrier Reef?" I ask Giselle for the tenth time.

She sits on the deck, lounging on the cushioned chair next to me, staring at the blue horizon. "Well, I want the tour but not from you. Someone else offered to take me. A local." Giselle adjusts her sunglasses on her nose and sips her fruity drink from her glass.

I push up my own sunglasses on my head, turning them into a headband to push the stray blond hair from my face. "A local?"

She holds a serious expression, pressing her lips together. "I've offered him surfing lessons, and he offered me the ocean." Her serious mouth splits as she beams a smile and then tips her head back to laugh. Her musical voice echoes through the air, and I just stare at her, processing the information.

"Giselle," I say. "Are you messing with me?"

"You never told me how persistent mermen are." She giggles, flipping her sunglasses on her head to finally look at me. "Sun's making me sushi later."

My mouth drops open. "What?"

She nudges me with the back of her hand. "It's just a date, Aves. Relax. He's nice...hot, too. We're not going to be asking for a coupling ceremony or anything."

"Yet," I say.

She covers her face with her hands, squealing. "This is all so crazy. But I do like him. Even all the gushy stuff."

I laugh. "Like how your hair captures the warmth of the sun?"

"Or how my eyes sparkle like the moonlight on rippling

tides?" she asks.

We look at each other and laugh again. I can't help it. I never dreamed Giselle would be interested in a merman who's just come to land. We've always just joked about her finding a merman mate.

Silence falls between us as I think about her possible future and how she could very well leave the coast of California for the aqua sea of Reefaria, so far from our home and my main colony of Pearlestria.

"I'm here for you if you ever need any advice," I say. "The mermaid life can be a hard adjustment."

She pats my knee. "I know. Relax, Aves. This is just one date."

"And you don't have to go through any transformation if you don't want to. You can love a merman and remain human," I say.

"So many options," she says. "I'm glad you changed the rules."

I lean over and hug Giselle. "Me, too."

Laughter sounds out from inside, and I tilt my head to look at everyone sitting and talking around the mound of crinkled wrapping paper scattered around the Christmas tree. Carter waves to me from his spot on the floor, a plate on his lap piled high with all the desserts we made together. His parents toast glasses of champagne with mine, and Luna shows Sapphire, Daisy, and Chloe how to weave a bracelet with fishing line, seashells, and sea glass. Christmas carols hum through the air, and I glance at the ocean sparkling with summer sunlight.

"Everything's ready on the beach," Bailey says, coming from the stairs.

I offer my hand out to Giselle and help her to her feet. Carter gets up from his spot and greets me with a kiss, holding my hand as we follow the others down the pathway that leads to the beach.

A Christmas tree sand sculpture stands tall in the sand, and tinsel shines from around the shady palms. Bailey passes out a bunch of Santa hats, and Matty and Logan motion for everyone to stand together for our obligatory Christmas photo.

Glancing at the water, I spot dozens of flickering sparks in the sea, the merpeople waiting for us to join them in the ocean.

"Say merry Christmas," Dad says, rushing to take his place next to Mom.

"Mer-Merry Christmas," Carter and I say together and then laugh.

The camera flashes, and Giselle bumps my hip, turning toward the water. A few heads pop up from the waves, and I wave my hand at the merpeople.

"So, are you sure you're okay with me going out with Sun?" Giselle asks, watching as the familiar merman emerges from the tide.

"You did want a merman for Christmas, didn't you?"

She grins and hugs me. "You're the best, Aves. This is the mer-merriest Christmas ever."

Dashing away, she splashes through the water. I smile at

Carter when Giselle hops on Sun's back and they dive into a wave. I catch sight of Luna watching Giselle, and then she beams a smile at me and joins my friends laughing on the beach.

"Ready for that special getaway I promised you?" Carter asks.

"Just you and me?" I ask.

He kisses me. "On land and in the sea."

"Always."

EPILOGUE

A NEW ADVENTURE

"YOU BETTER TEXT ME EVERY day," Giselle says. "I mean, like ten times a day."

I chuckle, handing the last box to Carter to put in my car. "We're just down the street, Gi."

"Yeah, which is so much farther than down the hall," she says.

I hug her. "I know, but I'm not going to miss you waking me up at the crack of dawn."

She taps my shoulder. "Don't think I won't still do that. I have a key."

I purse my lips, fake glaring. "Don't make me change the locks."

I squeeze my best friend once more, only pulling away at the sound of the back door sliding open. Luna steps onto the mat with a towel around her and a bag hanging from her fingertips. She looks around the small living room once before training her eyes on me and Giselle.

"Luna, you're just in time to kick Ava out," Giselle says with a laugh.

Luna bares her bottom teeth in a nervous grin. "I can't believe this is really happening."

"You're going to love it," I say, crossing the room to hug my mermaid friend. "Giselle is seriously the best to live with."

Giselle swipes her hand under her eye, smearing a tear. "You sure we can't just kick Carter out and have it be us three?"

"I don't think so," Carter says from the doorway. "No trying to steal my future wife."

Luna holds her hands over her heart and sighs.

Giselle puts her arm around Luna. "You two better not just disappear now that I can't keep an eye on you."

I throw my arms around Giselle and Luna. "You know we'll always return."

My essence might pull me to the sea, but Giselle and everyone I love will always tether me to the land.

"Come on, Aves," Carter says. "Mom and Dad are waiting at the shop."

"Enjoy your new adventure, Luna," I say, pulling away from my friends. "I'm sure it'll be a great one."

Giselle claps. "The best one ever."

~The End~

ACKNOWLEDGEMENTS

THIS BOOK WOULDN'T HAVE EXISTED if it weren't for two awesome people, who gave me the idea of taking my mermaids Down Under for a Christmas adventure—so thanks to Sarah Collier and Katie Harder-Schauer. You both made this book possible by extending your invaluable skills. Thanks to Sarah for helping me with the setting, the Aussie dialogue and slang, and for also introducing me to Pavlova. Thanks to Katie for giving me the idea of a mermaid solstice holiday and also for your endless excitement every time I send you a new project. Ta!

As always, thanks to my family and friends for their love and support. I wouldn't be where I am today if it weren't for each and every one of you.

Lastly, a huge thanks to those who took a chance on me. It means the world that you pick up and read my books. So thank you! I hope you enjoyed this magical mermaid adventure as much as I had.

❊ABOUT GINNA MORAN❊

GINNA MORAN IS A WRITER from sunny Southern California. She started writing poetry as a teenager in a spiral notebook that she still has tucked away on her desk today. Her love of writing grew after she graduated high school, and she completed her first unpublished manuscript at age eighteen.

When she realized her love of writing was her life's passion, she studied literature at Mira Costa College in Northern San Diego. Besides writing novels, she was senior editor, content manager, and image coordinator for Crescent House Publishing Inc. for four years.

Aside from Ginna's professional life, she enjoys binge watching television shows, playing pretend with her daughter, and cuddling with her dogs. Some of her favorite things include chocolate, anything that glitters, cheesy jokes, and organizing her bookshelf.

Ginna Moran loves to hear from her readers so visit her online at www.GinnaMoran.com. You can also find her on Facebook, Twitter, Instagram, and Snapchat(@GinnaMoran). To stay up-to-date on new releases, sign up to her newsletter. You'll not only get a FREE story, but you'll be able to participate in monthly giveaways!

Ginna Moran is currently hard at work on her next novel.

Other Young Adult Novels by Ginna Moran

PARANORMAL
Destined for Dreams Series
Demon Within Series
Finding Nate Series
Going Ghostly Series
Spark of Life Series
When Souls Collide Series
Demon Watcher Series

CONTEMPORARY
Falling into Fame Series

STANDALONES
Life After Lila

9 781942 073895